KT-572-646

SNOWBOUND WITH A STRANGER

When Megan's boyfriend breaks up with her for another woman, she decides to go alone to the secluded cottage in Scotland that she'd booked as a romantic setting for their Christmas together. After spending a miserable few days alone, a knock comes at the door: Jamie, caught in a snowstorm and unable to get into the cottage he's rented nearby, is looking for help. Megan finds herself increasingly drawn to her charming, funny and handsome visitor — but will there be room for him in her life when the snow melts?

Books by Patricia Keyson
in the Linford Romance Library:

CHERRY BLOSSOM
TIME AFTER TIME
A FEAST OF SONGS
HOLIDAY ROMANCE

PATRICIA KEYSON

SNOWBOUND WITH A STRANGER

Complete and Unabridged

LINFORD
Leicester

First published in Great Britain in 2013

First Linford Edition
published 2015

Copyright © 2013 by Patricia Keyson
All rights reserved

*A catalogue record for this book is available
from the British Library.*

ISBN 978–1–4448–2513–8

Published by
F. A. Thorpe (Publishing)
Anstey, Leicestershire

Set by Words & Graphics Ltd.
Anstey, Leicestershire
Printed and bound in Great Britain by
T. J. International Ltd., Padstow, Cornwall

This book is printed on acid-free paper

1

The pounding on the door startled Megan, but she leapt up from the armchair and rushed to answer it. If that was Douglas she was ready for him. What did he think he was playing at?

'You came after all,' she cried.

'Er . . . '

Her anticipation turned to surprise. There was a stranger standing in the doorway, trying to shelter from the snow. She hung on to the door and stared at him. The man pulled his jacket collar tighter around his neck and huddled into it. 'It's freezing out here.'

'It's not much better inside,' grimaced Megan. 'What do you want?' She hoped he'd hurry up as she wanted to get back to the relative warmth of the room with the door firmly closed.

'I've leased the cottage next door for a couple of nights.' He shivered, nodding his head to the right. 'Only the key doesn't seem to be where it should be. There's no signal from my mobile so I can't get in touch with the owners.'

'No, the signals have been nonexistent since I've been here and there isn't a landline.' Megan knew about the lack of reception as she'd checked and rechecked her phone, hoping to hear something from Douglas. She eyed up the man in front of her, curious about him. She reckoned he was a bit older than her. He was hunched into inadequate clothing, with a knitted cap pulled down around his ears. His spectacles gave him a serious look, although his eyes crinkled as he caught her staring at him.

'I'm sure I've got the right place.' He held out a printout and Megan looked at it with interest.

'Yes, that's the cottage over there.' Megan remembered the cottage from when she'd arrived, and hoped desperately it would be the one she'd rented as it was a good deal newer and smarter than the one she now occupied.

'The windows are double-glazed and so is the door,' the stranger informed her, 'so there's no way I can break in even if I thought it was a good idea. I don't suppose you know anything about it? Or have a spare key?'

Megan shook her head. 'I bet it's got central heating. If you can get in, I'm coming with you!' They exchanged another smile. 'You could drive into the village and see if anyone knows anything, I suppose.'

He shook his head. 'My car gave up, I'm afraid. Just coasted into a snowdrift and now it's stuck. Never mind, I'll go and give it another go, see if I can reverse out or something.'

'Good luck. I hope you get it going.'

'Me too.' He straightened his woollen hat. 'I'm Jamie, by the way, although we'll probably not see each other again.'

Taken aback at his introduction, she said, 'I'm Megan. Sorry not to have been able to help.'

Megan quickly closed the door

behind him so as not to lose any more of the precious heat from the fire which was sending puffs of smoke into the room. It really was a bitter evening. She sat warming herself, but couldn't get the guy out of her mind. Instead of offering him shelter she'd let him brave the elements. He might never get back down the lane to his car; he might freeze to death out there. She stood up and wandered nervously round the room, then kicked at her suitcase.

'What have I done?' she said aloud. She was surprised at herself. Her parents had always welcomed people into their home and she'd grown up feeling that was the right thing to do. But she knew she'd have to be out of her mind to consider inviting a stranger in. She tried to forget him, but found it impossible. Pictures of a frozen corpse found in a car at the end of the track formed in her brain and stayed there. There was only one course of action. She'd have to go down the lane and make sure he'd driven off safely.

Having made the decision she hurriedly pulled on a fleece, threw on her coat, wrapped a scarf round her neck, shoved on a hat and finished the outfit with thick woollen gloves. Finally she slipped her feet into her wellies. This time when she opened the door a gust of wind swept it out of her hands. Yanking hard, she managed to close it, then set off down the lane. The snow was deep and still falling thick and fast. Huge flakes gusted round her as she forced her way towards the road, every step requiring a vast effort.

'Jamie!' she called, but her voice was lost in the wind. 'Jamie!' she shouted. She hadn't brought a torch and, although the landscape was white, visibility was poor and she could barely see an arm's length in front of her. She was beginning to feel horribly, numbingly cold when there suddenly right in front of her was a car. It was an old wreck from what she could see; no wonder it had given up and sought sanctuary in a snowdrift.

She banged on the door. 'Jamie, are you in there? Jamie?' She tried the door, but it was locked. 'Jamie!' There was no response. He must have got lost making his way down to the car. 'Stupid, stupid man,' she said angrily, hitting the car with her fists. Pulling herself together, she set off back up the lane. It took a great deal of effort to make headway against the wind and all the way she called and peered through the swirling snow to see if she could make out a dark outline that might be Jamie.

The cottage loomed ahead and relief flooded through her. Once inside, she leant back against the door and it was only then that she let the tears flow. Why had she come to this wretched place alone? She made her way to the fire, which was still smoking badly and warmed herself, allowing the snow to melt from her clothes and form a puddle on the rug. She didn't know what to do.

If only Douglas hadn't ended their relationship and was here to look after her as originally planned. She tried to imagine his reassuring presence. What would he say? 'Come along now, Megan, people make their own choices. If that young fool wants to freeze to death that's up to him. He's not your responsibility.'

Sniffing back her tears and wiping her face with a damp sleeve, she realised that if Jamie found he was unable to go back the way he'd come, then she wouldn't be able to get out either. Also, she wasn't completely convinced that her little car would start after being left in the freezing conditions since late on Christmas Eve when she'd arrived here.

Tentatively, she reached for her phone. Who could she ring when the signal returned, if it ever did? Douglas wouldn't want to hear from her; she wasn't ready to go into details about her lost romance to her friends; and her mum, dad and sister were abroad in the more enjoyable warmth of Spain.

Her finger pressed the on button and

she waited, hoping she'd be able to think of someone to get her out of here. She waited longer than usual and waggled the instrument up and down, hoping to spark it into life. Nothing happened. She peered at the little screen; still no signal. How typical: she'd wanted a place far from everything and everyone, and that was exactly what she'd got.

In frustration, she flung the phone onto the settee which also served as her bed. What a miserable finale to her retreat over the jolly Christmas holidays — she was more than likely responsible for the disappearance, if not death, of Jamie. Surely he couldn't have got lost between the cottage and the car.

A loud thumping on the door made her jump. She jerked it open and there was Jamie, not frozen to death, but very much alive. He rubbed his hands together. 'I can't go anywhere tonight. There's so much snow the car won't move. I don't like to ask, but I thought you might give me something to eat, then I'll take it to the car and sleep there.'

'Where on earth were you?' cried Megan. 'I went hunting for you and you were nowhere to be seen. I yelled loud enough to wake the dead.'

Jamie looked awkward. 'Why would you do that? You don't even know me. I went to see if there was another house further up the road. Even if you'd used a loudhailer I doubt I'd have heard you. I didn't mean to put you to any trouble.'

Megan pointed inside the room at the sodden rug. 'That's the result of being deluged with snow and coming back here to thaw out.'

'You shouldn't have gone outside, it's treacherous,' Jamie said admonishingly. Then he softened. 'But it was a kind thing to do.'

'Possibly, or simply daft,' Megan exclaimed, feeling a bit foolish. 'I thought you were dead in the snow.' She wasn't an actress for nothing. Weren't her friends and family constantly telling her that she tended towards the dramatic? Then a thought struck her. She narrowed her eyes at him. 'If you were expecting to stay here, why didn't you bring any food?' Aha, what would he say to that?

'The owners said they'd arrange for a hamper of stuff to be left, so even if there is food it will be inside. Inside the locked cottage.'

Several degrees below zero spurred Megan into making a decision: probably not the most sensible in her life, but she couldn't let Jamie wander off again exposed to the elements with night almost upon them. If he was a mad axe murderer, so what? Did she care? Things couldn't be much worse than they had been during the last few days. Come to think of it, he hadn't barged his way in and was still standing politely on the doorstep, his ridiculous hat pushed down over his eyes with an accumulation of snow.

'No doubt I'll regret this, but do you want to come in?'

'Yes. But are you sure it's a good

idea? You're on your own, right?'

Megan was too cold and fed up to stand on the doorstep for much longer. 'Just come in. And shut the door behind you.' She shrugged off her saturated coat, scarf and gloves and left them in a pile on the rug, mentally telling herself she must try and dry them out later.

Jamie hesitated, then strode across the threshold and the door banged. He took off his jacket and collected the damp pile Megan had created. 'It's good of you to let me in. I'm grateful to have shelter and I'll try not to be a bother. I can't thank you enough.' He smiled at her and his eyes twinkled. 'Where can these go?' He looked around the small room, frowning. Megan was surprised how practical he was being. Very different to Douglas, who would have expected to be waited on hand and foot, although Megan doubted he would have looked as at home in the cottage as Jamie.

'Bathroom, I suppose. It's a very tiny

cottage,' replied Megan. She opened a cupboard next to the settee. 'There are a couple of hangers in here. You'll just have to drape things over the shower rail, if they're not too heavy.' Keeping busy and being in charge made her feel better. 'Then you can put some more wood on the fire. I brought in a load this morning, but only enough to last twenty-four hours.' A brief thought of the axe outside the door made her shudder a little as, for a moment, she imagined this spirited guy wielding it and doing her in. Bringing herself back to reality, she glanced at her packed bags and realised she didn't need to tell him her plans to leave first thing tomorrow. Although it was looking unlikely that she'd be able to leave after all.

Both of them worked independently, moving around each other as they got on with their appointed chores. Megan felt she had the biggest challenge, which was to find something for them to eat; the cupboards were practically bare.

When she'd been on her own, she'd eaten frugally as her broken heart dictated. Now, with company and the unexpected adventure of looking for bodies in the snow, she was ravenous.

'I'll give you a hand in here, shall I?' enquired Jamie, poking his head into the tiny kitchen. 'All the wet stuff's hanging up, but I think it'll take a while to dry out. I've put more logs on the fire. It's getting warmer already.'

'That's good. Unfortunately there's not much food,' said Megan, her stomach rumbling at the sound of the word. 'I was supposed to have a welcome hamper as well, but it didn't get here and I didn't bring any supplies with me, so we've only got the things a previous occupant left.' She opened cupboard after cupboard, almost hoping to magic provisions from thin air. 'Oh, look,' she exclaimed, 'what's that up there? It looks like it could be packets of something.' She jerked out a kitchen stool and began clambering on it to reach the high shelf.

'Let me,' said Jamie. Megan shot him

a look which would have silenced any other man, but he blundered on. 'Please,' he begged, 'let me do something useful.'

Jamie knelt on the stool and handed down the contents from the top of the cupboard. Megan laid out the supplies on the short worktop. Jamie pushed the stool away so there was room for the two of them to stand side by side in the kitchen. Together they inspected their hoard.

Megan sighed. 'Not exactly inspiring, is it?'

'Come on, Delia Smith,' grinned Jamie, 'something tasty will come out of that lot. It's just a case of creativity.'

'I suppose you're Jamie Oliver in disguise,' she returned, looking hard at him. 'Actually, in a certain light . . . no, you look nothing like him.' With the thought of a hot meal to look forward to they both giggled, united in hunger. 'Packet soup and a tin of hotdogs. How does that sound? Good job it's got a ring-pull top. There's no tin opener.'

'Are you sure?' asked Jamie.

'Have a look yourself. If you can find one, I'll gladly use it. There are loads of tins if we only had a tin opener.'

'Okay, I take your word for it,' said Jamie. 'Can we have the pasta as well?'

'Better leave that for tomorrow,' said Megan sensibly. 'After all, we don't know how long we'll be here for, do we?'

Her words cast a cloud over them and Jamie wandered off to stoke the fire.

* * *

'Delicious,' pronounced Jamie, putting his spoon and fork into his empty dish. 'I could include that in my next recipe book.'

Megan grinned, spooning up the last of her meal. 'You've done well with the fire. I'm feeling quite cosy now.' She yawned widely. 'It's been a long day.' Things were turning out okay, although she knew she'd been rash to make a decision which might not have had such a good result. The fact that Douglas would have been horrified cheered her up no end!

Jamie got to his feet. 'I'll wash these dishes up and then I'll be on my way.'

'What do you mean? You're not going out tonight. That's madness.'

'I said I'd sleep in the car,' protested Jamie. 'I don't want you to feel you've got to put me up as well as feed me. You wouldn't have a lot of privacy in this, er . . . compact cottage if I stayed, would you?'

Megan listened to the clattering in the kitchen. If he was an ill-intentioned mad axe murderer, she'd have been attacked by now; and if there was anything worth stealing in the cottage and among her luggage, he could have it. When he returned clutching his jacket and hat, she tried to persuade him. 'You're welcome to stay. It would be foolish to venture out in that awful weather.'

But Jamie pulled on his still-damp

jacket, rammed his woolly hat on his head and set off towards the car. Megan watched him go with a sinking heart, hoping he'd be safe and comfortable.

2

After a half hour into reading her book, Megan's yawns increased. If Jamie hadn't called she'd probably be in bed by now in preparation for her early start. Then she remembered the snow and that there was no way she would be able to leave early tomorrow, Jamie or no Jamie. Getting ready for bed, Megan turned the tap in the bathroom. The water came out in drops rather than a gush and she realised the pipes must have frozen in the last couple of hours. Grappling in her sponge bag, she pulled out a packet of damp tissues and used them to wash herself. She studied her reflection in the mirror. She'd been told often enough she was pretty in the past, and her layered blond hair usually looked good. Megan thought she looked a little like Kirsten Dunst, but Douglas had compared her to a grim-faced newsreader on the BBC news. She was quite proud of her figure — trim, but nicely curved.

Megan wondered why she hadn't seen the brush-off coming.

'What a peculiar idea to have Christmas in isolation,' he'd said during their last meeting together. 'Typical of you, Megan.'

'It'll be so romantic,' Megan returned dreamily, ignoring his apathy. 'Just the two of us.'

'I can't make it for more than a few days, though,' he said, taking out his tablet and consulting it. 'What day did you say we're going? It can't be before Christmas Eve. I've meetings right up until then.'

Ever the optimist, Megan decided to book the cottage right through to New Year in the hope that once there he could be tempted to stay for longer. She tried to get him into a more romantic mood. Her arms wound around him and she tried to pull him close.

'Don't crease my shirt,' Douglas had

reacted, pushing her away gently and straightening his tie. 'I've an important appointment so I'll have to go now.' He had briefly kissed her cheek before leaving.

Megan swept away thoughts of Douglas as she brought herself back to the present. It was difficult to clean her teeth, but she managed a cursory brush. The idea of undressing appalled her so she chose to sleep dressed as she was. It was an arduous task to change the settee into a bed, but it had proved quite comfortable on the other nights. Her mind was racing as she thought of Jamie. He was a fool to spend the night in the car, but she'd offered him shelter and he'd refused it. She should clear him from her mind. Lying in bed with blankets piled over her and her head partially under the pillow, she thought sleep would come easily. Yet gazing into the flickering fire she was surprised that she kept seeing images of Jamie. Firmly she told herself that it was only because she'd been deprived of human company over the last few days. Gradually her eyelids drooped and she drifted off into sleep.

* * *

Megan awoke with icy feet and a cold nose. A couple of her blankets had fallen off the bed and the fire was completely dead. Her thoughts flew to Jamie; if she was cold with a roof and several layers over her, then how was he faring? She tottered to the window and tried to glimpse the weather conditions outside, but the misted-up glass and dark night sky prevented her seeing anything.

She patiently laid the fire again and lit it, telling herself that the wood would catch soon and she'd be lovely and warm. While she was waiting, she re-made her bed and tucked everything in so that she had a snug cocoon awaiting her. Among the crackles and pops of the fire, Megan was sure she heard a knock at the door. Was it Jamie coming back? After running to investigate the possibility, the only thing she saw outside the door was snow. No tracks to or from the cottage. There'd been a fresh fall after Jamie had left for the night.

Megan's mobile phone lay on the kitchen worktop and she fiddled with it, knowing in her heart that there'd still be no signal. And she was right. If there had been a signal, Megan knew she'd get in touch with Douglas, which would have been a big mistake. She could just imagine what he'd say.

'You're not telling me you're in the wilds of Scotland on your own? Whatever were you thinking?'

'It was booked and I wanted to be away from everyone being jolly at Christmas,' she'd reply.

'I suggest you go back to your flat at once.'

'I can't. I'm snowed in. What shall I do, Douglas? Please help me.' Megan cringed as a pathetic needy speech played in her head. It dawned on her that she was only like this with Douglas.

Automatically, she lifted the kettle and held it under the kitchen tap, momentarily forgetting about the frozen pipes. A cup of tea would have been welcome, but there was no way she could have one now. She studied the provisions that were left. To the pile she added the tins that couldn't be opened. Perhaps she should write a cookery column about how to survive in a snowed-up cottage miles from anywhere with no water, precious little food and no tin opener.

A smile broke the despair on her features and she walked her fingers across the formica. How could she have missed that? A packet of chocolate digestives hiding among the mound of packets dug out by Jamie. A feast. Cramming two of the delicious biscuits into her mouth, she savoured the taste, crunching happily. Never had chocolate been so welcome. When thoughts of Jamie reared themselves once again, she sighed deeply. She would have to go and find him; there was no way she'd be able to rest or even enjoy another biscuit without knowing he was safe.

Rummaging through her suitcase, she pulled out several items. Having hurriedly thrown on an outfit of all the dry clothes she had, and with a blanket wrapped around her, Megan set out once more to find Jamie's car. How could he be so selfish as to make her come out to unearth him?

Willing herself on with thoughts that as soon as the thaw came she'd be out of this desolate place and back to civilisation, she surmised that she could only blame herself for choosing to descend alone into this wilderness in the first place. There's always a man behind bad things that happen, she told herself. If Douglas had come away with her as they'd planned, things would have been different. Her pace increased as she thought how he would have reacted to Jamie's arrival at the cottage. But Douglas wasn't here; he'd chosen to be somewhere else.

She lumbered towards the car and

banged on the window, trying to peer in, but could see nothing. 'Jamie, are you in there?' she yelled. If he was alive, he'd have heard her, she was sure. 'Jamie,' she cried again, 'please answer me.' *And please be all right*, she added to herself.

As she toyed with the idea of smashing the windows, she heard a slight sound. Alert now, she listened again. The surroundings were silenced by the snow. What she'd heard must have been some animal scurrying for safety and shelter. Then she heard it again. Putting her ear next to the car door, she held her breath. Not knowing whether to laugh or cry, she got angry. 'Jamie, you beast, how could you be fast asleep and snoring when I'm worried sick about you?'

At last Megan's yells were rewarded with a reply. The window creaked, but was too frozen to wind down. An outline appeared as Megan stared into the car. 'Is that you, Meg?'

'Of course it's me,' she replied. 'Who

on earth else could it be?'

'The window's stuck. Hang on, I'll try and open the door.'

Now Megan knew that Jamie was safe, she tried to calm down. She'd been very worried and acknowledged that she wanted Jamie to be all right, and he was. As she took a couple of deep, icy breaths, Jamie forced open a rear door and beamed up at her. 'Did you think I was dead again?'

Miserably, Megan nodded her head. Then she peered into the car. Luke-warm air wafted out and Jamie was wrapped up in a sleeping bag. He'd been quite comfortable while she'd worried. She turned to trudge back. 'Sorry to have disturbed you,' she murmured.

As the cottage appeared in front of her, she heard a shout from behind. 'Meg, Meg.'

Gritting her teeth at the name he seemed determined to call her, she didn't stop, but slowed her pace a little until Jamie caught up with her.

'It was thoughtful of you to be concerned. What are you doing awake so early in the morning?'

'What time is it?' enquired Megan.

'Half two,' replied Jamie.

With her front door open, Megan said, 'Do you want to come in?'

'Yes, please.' Jamie trailed his sleeping bag across the threshold and pulled off his woollen hat.

Megan gave a cheeky grin as she beckoned him into the kitchen. 'See? Chocolate biscuits.' She waited for Jamie's reaction.

'Gosh, it's good of you to invite me to your coffee morning, but I'm still full from supper.'

'*Are* you?'

'No,' spluttered Jamie, making a grab for the crinkly packet and holding it out for Megan to take a biscuit.

'I've had one or two already,' she said, taking another.

'Really?' He grinned at her. 'So, are you going to offer me tea, or do I have to make it myself?'

'There's no water; the pipes are frozen.'

'It's obvious you were never a boy scout. Do you know what all that white stuff out there is made of?' Jamie asked, taking a pan and heading for the door. 'I'll fill this up and we'll soon have a delicious brew.'

Megan felt foolish. The cold and isolation must be addling her brain. She must get away from here as soon as she possibly could.

Minutes later, Jamie was back in the kitchen cheerfully whistling and bustling around finding mugs and spoons.

'I can't bear people who are cheerful first thing in the morning,' Megan said, as she drifted back into the living room. She stabbed at the fire with the poker, hoping to stir some more life into it.

Jamie followed her in, carrying the steaming mugs. 'Well, we're both up now so we might as well make the most of it.'

Megan sat in the armchair and cupped her hands round the mug, trying to draw some warmth from it. 'I'm freezing. Were you really comfortable in your car?'

Jamie perched on the arm of her chair. 'Not exactly, but I knew I had to get on with it so I put on all the clothes I have with me and it wasn't too bad. My sleeping bag's one of those for extreme conditions. I only bought it because it was in a sale. I was pretty shattered after the awful drive I had yesterday, so it wasn't difficult falling asleep.' He paused. 'You know, you remind me of someone. Who is it? I can't remember now, but it'll come to me.'

Megan hoped it wouldn't come to him. She didn't want him to think she was anything like the shameless woman she'd played in the popular TV soap *Watch Your Back*.

What was it Douglas had said? 'Really, Megan, you should give up this acting nonsense if that's the only sort of part you can get. You'll definitely have to give it up when we get married and have children. We don't want them to be teased because their mother played a slut on television.'

Sitting in companionable silence now, she asked herself if Jamie would have the same reaction and why she should care. She glanced sideways. The strange thing was that something about him attracted her. He had looked a bit nerdy with his woollen hat pulled over his head and ears and his spectacles steamed up, but sitting an arm's length from her, relaxing, he looked pretty good. His dark hair curled around his ears and his cocoa-brown eyes sparkled when he spoke. She also liked the enthusiasm with which he approached almost any task. He didn't put off going out in the freezing conditions and was happy to lend a hand in the kitchen. Supposing he was going to end up as a short-term lodger, she couldn't have chosen anyone better, she concluded.

If Douglas had come to this cottage with her, how would he have fared in these sub-zero temperatures with no water and precious little heat? She almost laughed out loud at the thought of Douglas making do in such primitive conditions.

'There's no way I can stay here,' Douglas would say. 'The whole set-up is unbelievable. A hut to stay in, meagre rations, and not even running water. I'll draft a letter of complaint to the owners with a threat to sue them, especially as you booked a cottage with two bedrooms and we've ended up with this. They'll soon give us our money back and maybe some compensation as well.'

Just wait until she got home and told her friends that instead of spending an exciting Christmas week in a love nest in the highlands of Scotland with Douglas, she'd almost frozen to death with a complete stranger who tugged at her heartstrings. No, that was too ridiculous. It must be the lack of sleep.

'I'm turning in,' she said. 'Will you be okay in the armchair?'

'If you're sure it's all right for me to stay in the cottage with you. We *are* both decently clothed.' Jamie stood and looked down at himself. 'More Michelin Man than Superman. Would you like something else to eat before we go to sleep? I'm so hungry I could eat a haggis if we could catch one,' he joked.

'Ha! As you know there isn't much *to* eat. Why don't you just finish off the biscuits?'

'If you don't mind, I will.'

* * *

'Are you awake?' Jamie whispered into the darkness.

'Yes, I'm still freezing. It must have been coming out to fetch you back. I can't warm up.' Megan shivered.

'I thought I could hear you tossing and turning. This armchair's as lumpy as my gran's porridge. I'm not complaining.'

'Not much, you're not,' Megan giggled.

'It's just that the springs keep digging into me even through the five T-shirts, three jumpers, a fleece, jacket and sleeping bag.'

'Gosh, you must be really thin under all that!'

'Wait until we've been trapped here for weeks. There'll be nothing left of us.'

'That's not funny.' Megan didn't want to be trapped in a freezing cottage with no food, running water or contact with the outside world. Even if she was with a lovely man.

'You know I still can't remember where I've seen you before. I think it might be somebody in my department at uni who looks like you.'

'Jamie . . . ' Megan really wasn't sure she should ask this.

'Yes, Meg, I know, you want me to shut up so that you can get some sleep.'

'No, I want to ask you something, but I'm a bit embarrassed.'

'Let me guess, you want to borrow my woolly hat.'

'No.' Here goes, she thought to herself. 'I wondered if we could sleep back to back to keep us warmer. I read it in a book years ago. What do you think?'

There was a silence.

'Jamie, I just meant for warmth,' she apologised. 'Please forget it.' Megan squirmed and felt her face at least growing warmer even if the rest of her was icy cold.

'No, I'd be honoured. It's not every day a beautiful woman falls for my charms and asks me to be her hot-water bottle. I'll just shuffle over and you'll soon be as warm as toast.'

And it was true. With Jamie curled up in his sleeping bag next to her, she soon began to thaw and drift off to sleep, albeit with the thought that if she was sensible she wouldn't be in this position. Her family and friends would be appalled if they knew.

She was suddenly wakened by Jamie's voice right in her ear. 'I know where I've seen you before! You were Amy in *Watch Your Back*. Killed off in a car accident. Poor you.' Jamie turned over and put his arm round her to give her a hug. 'Never mind. Nothing terrible is going to happen to you with me here.' He rolled back over again, getting completely tangled up in his sleeping bag. 'Night, night.'

Megan tossed and turned. Whilst anxious not to disturb Jamie, she was starting to get cold again.

'We could play I Spy,' said Jamie, the sound of his voice startling Megan.

'I thought you were asleep,' she said. 'And how can we play I Spy in the dark?'

'Fair point,' replied Jamie. 'How about a word game? I say a word, like panini, and you have to think of a word beginning with the last letter.'

'Idiot,' said Megan immediately.

'Toast.'

'Tagliatelle.'

'Entrecôte steak.' Jamie smacked his lips. 'We'll never get to sleep thinking about food. I'll tell you a story, shall I? Get yourself comfortable. Once upon a time there was . . . '

Megan was soon lulled into a deep sleep, now nice and secure beside Jamie.

3

When Megan woke later that morning, the sun was streaming through the windows. It took her a few minutes to take in her surroundings and remember where she was. And who was with her.

She turned and took in every detail of Jamie's face. His enviably long lashes cast a shadow on his flushed cheeks, and a growth of dark stubble had developed overnight, giving him a quixotic look which even Colin Firth would envy. Megan fantasised for a couple of seconds about what would happen if the snow never melted and she and Jamie had to live side by side like this forevermore. A smile curled her mouth as she speculated as to whether she'd be able to put up with it. With her face close to his, she could feel his gentle breath on her cheeks. Snuggling back under the covers, she felt cosy and safe. If they weren't able to get away from the cottage today, staying here in bed seemed a good option.

Jamie stirred and mumbled something.

'What did you say?' Megan asked.

'Where am I?'

She was just able to make out what he was saying and laughed. 'In the middle of nowhere,' she informed him.

'Oh good.' He settled again and she could barely resist stroking his face.

If Douglas could see her now, what would he think? Why should she care? He was the past and there was no reason she shouldn't do just what she liked and share her bed, however innocently, with whoever she chose to. Feeling pleased that she could think about her split from Douglas in this slightly rebellious way, she peeked at the fire and groaned. There was just a small glow and all the wood she'd brought in yesterday had been used up. She'd have to go out and get some more.

Trying to make as little disturbance as possible she slid out of bed, wrapped a blanket round her shoulders, put on her wellies and opened the door to be greeted by the sight of yet more snow. It was piled so deeply in places she wasn't sure she'd be able to make her way to the wood store.

Then she felt Jamie's comforting arm round her shoulders. 'Let me get the wood. Just point me in the right direction. As soon as I get back we'll have breakfast and then think about what we're going to do.'

Megan stood a moment longer enjoying the view. It was an almost alpine scene with the sun glinting on the snow, which covered everything in sight. There was an unbelievable stillness and silence; she'd never thought there could be such a silence.

The sight of Jamie lugging a container full of logs brought her back to their predicament. She hurried back inside to fetch a pan so that she could make a hot drink. Whilst the water was boiling she checked the supplies for a possible breakfast. A packet of out-of-date cereal seemed the best choice, although they would have to eat it dry.

With the fire roaring and the two of them sitting up in bed tucking into their bowls of cereal, they chatted.

'Is there some particular reason why you came to stay in this isolated cottage without much food?' Jamie asked.

'I didn't bring *any* food. The stuff that's in the kitchen was already here.'

'Right. Is there some particular reason why you came to stay in this isolated cottage without bringing any provisions?'

'Seems crazy, doesn't it? We . . . I ordered all the stuff I'd need and it was supposed to be delivered on Christmas Eve, the day I arrived, but it didn't turn up. I was going to drive to the village shop then, but the roads were icy and I decided it wasn't worth risking. And after that the snow kept getting worse and worse. I know I should have made the effort before it got really bad, but I couldn't be bothered. Not just for me.'

'So you've been stuck here on your own living on a meagre diet for three or four days? Over the festive season, too.' Jamie frowned.

'Yes, but as you can see — ' She pointed towards her open bags and case. ' — I was all ready to leave first thing and had my suitcase packed. It's all a bit of a mess now, as I had to get more clothes out when I came looking for you.' They both looked at her other bits and pieces strewn across the floor. 'What are we going to do?'

'Tidy up? I think first of all I should go to my car and bring my Christmas gifts back. This cereal's past it. It tastes musty. We must ration ourselves though.'

'That's funny. You're the one who finished off the biscuits last night. We could be having those for breakfast instead of this miserable muesli.' She didn't want to sound petulant, but she longed for another chocolate digestive.

'Got it! Jam's the answer. I saw jam in the kitchen. If we mix it in with the cereal it will taste delicious.' Jamie leapt out of bed and was soon back with the jar of jam. He spooned some into their bowls and they both stirred it in before sampling the mix.

'Mmmm. Strawberry cereal surprise, see how good it is.' Jamie tucked in.

'Much better. Start your day with Jamie's jammy joy.' Megan was glad Jamie was here with her to share the ups and downs. She'd thought being on her own would be therapeutic, but she'd been miserable and lonely.

'You could be in the advert for it. You did that one for yoghurts, didn't you? It was really clever. I liked the friendly bacteria in it too, and you were just brilliant in the soap; I couldn't believe it when they killed you off. Wait until I tell my mates I've shared Amy's bed, just like all the other blokes in Leeds.'

'Don't you dare! There definitely won't be an invite tonight if you carry on like this. It will be back to the car for you.'

Jamie balanced his bowl in his lap and put his arm round Megan to give her a hug. 'I can't believe I'm saying this, but I'm very glad I got snowed in here. Only because you're here. Although if we don't get out soon, I am likely to miss the best Hogmanay party ever. Loads of my friends will be there. I rented the cottage to have a few days to myself before revving up again. But I have to say that although I didn't get the rest I'd envisaged, I'm having a great time!'

'I hope we get out soon. In spite of your enthusiasm for my work, my career's on a downward spiral. I gave up the chance of being Snow White in a panto to come here for the week, and if I'm still stuck here next week I'm going to miss the audition for a major advertising company.'

'We could always be rescued somehow.'

'Dream on. There's no signal here.'

'I know; I've tried my phone again. No, I meant flares or signs in the snow,' said Jamie.

'And just how many helicopters have you seen flying over who would spot our message? And just where do we find the flares?' She felt unkind to dampen his eagerness.

'Spoilsport.'

'Do you watch a lot of adventure films by any chance?' Megan asked.

'I've seen one or two. But I'd watch any type of film with you in it. That's a point. I suppose we have to make our own entertainment as we have no TV. We'll have to play charades and word games on paper. A bit like we did last night — or early this morning, I suppose it was. That's what we used to do when I was younger. We'd have these big family Christmas parties with all our relatives and play loads of different games. Is there a radio?' Jamie looked round the room.

'There's a very small one. Reception's not good and I think the batteries are running low, but I did listen to the news and weather a couple of times. I suppose we ought to try and catch the weather report to see when it might improve.'

'Good idea. Anything else we need to do today?'

'We ought to check the wood pile. Some of the wood is cut up, but we may need to chop some more. Are you any good with an axe?' Megan's head flew up at the thought of something sinister happening, but Jamie was innocently throwing a log on the fire. She chided herself for being so fanciful. 'And we'll need to heat up some water for washing. It's going to be so horrible not being able to have showers, and my hair's going to be such a mess. Perhaps we'll be able to wash our hair using pans of water.'

'In a day or two we won't be able to get near each other! We'd better make the most of it.' He took Megan's dish and piled it with his own on the floor, then settled back in his sleeping bag. 'Let's have another sleep. All this messing about in the night, physical work and lack of food is too much. We can do our chores this afternoon.'

Megan didn't have a better suggestion

to make, and this was the cosiest place in the cottage. The fire was glowing, the sun was streaming through the window, and she was perfectly happy to sleep back to back sharing warmth with Jamie, an almost stranger.

* * *

Megan woke from a dreamless sleep and stretched her limbs. Heat coursed through her and she savoured the feeling before opening her eyes. The other side of the bed was empty. She'd kill that Jamie if he'd gone off without letting her know. Throwing off the covers and regretfully leaving the comfort of the bed, she poked at the waning fire. She looked around the dishevelled room and then immersed herself in a spot of housework.

Douglas would be proud of her. One of his favourite phrases was, 'Tidy surroundings mean a tidy mind.' But he wouldn't be very impressed by her attire. 'You should always look your best; you never know who's going to call and what opportunity you might miss if you're still in your slippers and rollers.'

She giggled. She didn't think Jamie would mind much if she had rollers in and was wearing a hair net. He'd just make fun of her in his silly way until they were both laughing. She resolved to put Douglas out of her mind as much as she could because thinking about him didn't make her happy. Her thoughts returned to Jamie. Wherever he'd gone, Megan convinced herself that he would be back.

After cleaning the tiny kitchen and sweeping the lino floor, she lined up the possibilities of food for the next meal. The energy she'd used had made her hungry. She was surprised how she was now governed by the need for warmth and food. The snow couldn't last forever; they'd be able to leave soon, she told herself.

As she was now quite content and happy, she took the washing-up bowl and a large saucepan outside and filled them up with snow. A narrow, icy path had been dug in the snow from the front door of the cottage, disappearing in the direction of Jamie's car. He was certainly resourceful, she thought. Lifting the snow-filled containers, she saw a mound of cut logs piled high in the open-sided wood store. And he said he wasn't Superman, she murmured to herself, a smile on her face. Things were looking good.

'Meg! Meg!'

She turned and waited for Jamie, who was trudging along his self-made path carrying a bulging bag and a spade. He reached the cottage door, propped the spade up against the stone wall and bounded inside, leaving wet footprints.

'I've just cleaned that,' complained Megan, pulling her own boots off as she stepped inside. Her hand flew to her mouth. 'I can't believe I said that,' she giggled. 'I sound like my mum.' She pulled excitedly at his bag. 'What's in there?

Jamie grinned. 'I'd better leave my

shoes by the front door even if it means my feet turn to ice. Then we can have a sort through these things.' Standing on the cold floor he looked down and wriggled his toes, then glanced across at the wellies standing near the door. 'Those are fancy. It would be good if they're my size.'

Megan made a grab for them. 'They're mine,' she cried, hugging them to her chest. 'Good, aren't they? My sister gave them to me as an early Christmas present.' She held them out to be admired.

'You can have them,' grinned Jamie. 'Pink flowers on a yellow background aren't my thing this season.'

Megan headed for the kitchen and rummaged in a cupboard under the sink. 'I spotted these earlier. Would they fit you?' She held out a pair of faded black rubber boots.

Jamie looked at them doubtfully. 'Possibly. Thanks.'

They sat together in front of the fire which Jamie had coaxed into a roar of heat. 'Lucky dip,' said Jamie, holding out the bag.

Megan's hand hovered and then she delved straight in and pulled out a pair of socks with a rather rude message. 'Gross, you can have these.' She tossed them onto his lap.

'Thank you, kind lady. Considering these are my Christmas presents, you're very generous.'

Grabbing the bag, Megan held it up for Jamie. He hauled out a long black woolly scarf. 'Good old Gran,' he said, leaning over and winding it around Megan's neck. His hand brushed her cheek as he did so and Megan jumped at the softness of his touch. They sat gazing into each other's eyes. Jamie broke the spell by holding up the bag again. 'Your turn,' he whispered.

'This one hasn't been opened,' cried Megan, removing a small hard parcel wrapped in cheery Christmas paper.

'Must have missed that.'

'What is it?' She scrabbled at the package.

'Just what we need,' crowed Jamie. 'A tin and bottle opener together with a penknife and lots of other useful tools. My brother knows me well. He could have thrown in a Sat Nav too.' He was on his feet and out into the kitchen, closely followed by Megan. 'You can choose what we eat,' he said. 'What do you fancy?'

I think I fancy you, thought Megan. Out loud she said, 'All of it. I could eat all of it.'

Frowning, Jamie said, 'Well, you can't; we agreed to share.'

Megan swiped a hand at him. 'Idiot.' Then she inspected the tins. 'How about pasta and this tin of sauce?'

'Great. You cook the pasta then.' He held out a saucepan.

Megan put her hands on her hips. 'And what will you be doing while I'm doing that?' she demanded.

'Opening the tin, of course,' chuckled Jamie.

A short while later their plates were empty. The contents of tins of fruit cocktail and custard had been poured into dishes ready to be eaten.

'That was the tastiest meal I've ever had,' declared Jamie, patting his tummy. He glanced over at Megan and lifted his finger to her mouth. 'You've a spot of sauce just there,' he said.

Although he didn't actually physically touch her, Megan's insides were on fire. She moved herself away from him on the pretence of cleaning her face in the bathroom. While there, she did a tidy up, putting off going back to him. There was no way she could let him share her bed tonight. Was there? *Don't even go there*, she chided herself. Experimentally, she turned the tap. A small spurt of water chugged out and then stopped.

'My hair,' she wailed out loud after seeing her reflection in the mirror above the sink. Her fingers tried to ruffle it into something respectable, but failed. She couldn't put off joining Jamie any longer. Taking a deep breath, she trailed back to the living room.

'Guess what I've found,' said Jamie,

giving her a wide smile.

'Bar of chocolate?' That would be a good find.

'No. It's food, though.' Jamie handed over a tin to her.

Baffled, she prised off the lid. 'Wow. Christmas cake. You must have known you had that.' Megan looked into the tin. 'Just checking you haven't been nibbling it.'

'Would I do a thing like that? We're supposed to be sharing.' Jamie looked shocked.

'Like we shared the chocolate biscuits, you mean,' moaned Megan.

'You're not still thinking about those, are you?' He put his hands on her shoulders and looked down at her. 'You told me to finish them.'

Megan's chin lifted in defiance. 'And you did, didn't you. It was very selfish of you.'

Jamie let his hands fall from Megan and he took the tin into the kitchen. Megan felt ashamed; she shouldn't have said it. After all, he'd chopped wood as well as going out to his car to bring back things to share. He'd even donated his gran's Christmas gift to her. She caressed the soft scarf still around her neck. Selfish? No, he wasn't at all selfish. In fact, he was very kind and thoughtful and very good company; much better than Douglas, she admitted to herself. It would serve her right if Jamie left her. Not only would she be on her own; she wouldn't even have the luxury of a tin opener.

In the kitchen, Jamie was cutting the Christmas cake. 'Like some now?' he asked.

'I'm sorry,' mumbled Megan. 'I shouldn't have said that.'

Jamie shrugged and held out a piece of cake. 'I didn't forget about this, but I don't really go for fruit cake.'

Megan sunk her teeth into the fruity, moist slab and chewed. When she'd half-finished her slice, she said, 'No, I don't like Christmas cake, either.'

Crumbs choking her as she couldn't stop giggling, Jamie had to pat her on the back several times. With a flushed face and streaming eyes, Megan thought she'd never felt as happy as now. But she wouldn't let Jamie know that. She didn't want to make a fool of herself by appearing clingy.

Like she wasn't making a fool of herself now?

4

Megan relaxed in the chair by the fire reading, but Jamie couldn't settle. He kept jumping up, going to the window and peering out. 'No thaw yet,' he said. 'I'm not sure what we should do. Supposing it doesn't thaw for weeks? What do we do then? Do you think I should try to walk to the village and get someone to rescue you?'

'If you can get to the village, then I'm sure I can. I'm not some damsel in distress who needs a hero to rescue her.' *Or am I?* she thought. *Wouldn't I like Jamie to pick me up in his arms and sweep me off somewhere?*

'I know you're a very independent woman, but it would be something for me to do.'

'It's dark now. You can't go out. Please, don't even think about it. Oh, Jamie, don't you read? There's a stack of books on the shelf over there. Just choose one, sit down and stop fussing about going out. I can't bear the thought of it.'

'It's nice that you care.' Jamie laughed quietly before wandering over and pulling one book out after another. '*100 Crossword Puzzles*, *Dictionary of Quotations*, *Teach Yourself Dutch*, *An Introduction to Computers*, *Prize-Winning Slogans*. Not exactly holiday reading. What's in this cupboard?'

Megan put her bookmark in place and closed the book. There was no way she could concentrate with Jamie chattering away. Not that she minded. If it had been her sister or even Douglas, she would have been irritated. She watched as Jamie explored the cupboard. He reminded her of an excitable child who had just found treasure.

'Look at this lot. Board games! I challenge you to a game of Scrabble and Monopoly.'

'At the same time?'

'No, one at a time. Later this evening. After dinner. Have we had dinner?'

Megan chuckled. 'I'm not sure what meal it was we've just had, but I'll definitely need something else before we go to bed . . . I mean before bedtime.' Now she felt daft and embarrassed. He wouldn't have noticed what she'd said; he was too interested in the games. But now he was looking at her strangely.

'It's okay, Meg. If you're unhappy with the sleeping arrangements I can try the armchair again or even go back to the car.'

'No, it's silly. I mean I'm silly.'

'Yes, you are.'

Megan reached behind her and pulled out the cushion and threw it at him. It caught him squarely in the chest.

'Good shot!' Clutching the cushion, he moved across and sat on the arm of her chair. 'Will anyone be worried about you?'

'No, they all knew I was coming here for Christmas. Not that everybody was very happy about it. My brother wasn't bothered — he always does his own thing anyway; but we're good friends. My sister was a bit cross because we've never had Christmas apart before. Mum and Dad didn't say anything much, but I felt they were disappointed I didn't go to Spain with them. They said they hoped I'd have a good time. What about you? Will anyone be worried?'

'No one is expecting me to be anywhere until the Hogmanay party.'

'If you don't turn up for the party they might report you missing, and there'll be search parties all over Scotland looking for you. You might be on the front of the newspaper.' Megan knew she was being overdramatic again.

'Like you were when you slept with Mo's husband, Les, when she had to go into hospital?' he teased.

'That was fiction, Jamie. I was acting a part.'

'And now that I've met you I know what a very good actress you are. You're nothing like Amy at all. I wish I could watch you as Snow White. You'd have to improve on your housekeeping skills for that role. Those books are very dusty and I thought you'd been cleaning up whilst I was doing all the manly tasks.' He reached over and kissed the top of her head. Then he leapt up. 'I don't know why I did that. Forgive me?'

'It's okay,' she said quietly. *It's more than okay*, she thought.

Jamie was over by the window again. 'I expect it was just the Christmas spirit taking over. You kiss everyone at Christmas, don't you? Old wrinkled aunts smelling of lavender, babies with their dinner on their faces or who've just been sick, old uncles with bad breath . . . '

'Stop! I know my hair's bad, but comparing me to a baby who's been sick . . . '

'I've put my foot in it again. I shouldn't have said that. What's in these carrier bags?'

'My Christmas presents. I brought them with me. I was going to unwrap them on Christmas Day, but it didn't seem much fun on my own.'

'What *did* you do on Christmas Day?' Jamie asked.

'Nothing much. I read my book, stoked the fire and had a tin of baked beans. I hadn't thought what a clever idea those ring-pull cans are until I came here. It wasn't exactly the best Christmas Day I've ever had. Shall I open my presents now?'

'Hold on. I just need to fetch something.' Jamie rushed from the room, letting in an icy cold draught. He was soon back waving a large frond of conifer. 'Our Christmas tree! I'll wedge it here between these books.'

'That's so lovely.' Megan was once again surprised at Jamie's actions. He clearly had the ability to turn an ordinary occasion into something special. 'Are you ready? Can we start?'

'Here's a pretty one with fancy

ribbon,' Jamie said, pulling a gift out of the bag. 'Somebody's taken a lot of care. Let's see. 'From Douglas with love. I hope in time you'll move forward and be able to forgive me. It's for the best.''

Megan leapt up and snatched the present from him. 'Leave it,' she shouted. She pushed it back into the carrier bag.

'It's like treading on eggshells with you, Meg. I'm just being myself. I'm going for a walk, whether you like it or not.'

* * *

Sitting in the darkness by the fire, Megan wished she hadn't been so touchy, especially after Jamie's thoughtful gesture with the tree. It wasn't his fault that Douglas had given her a Christmas gift. It was the comment about him taking a lot of care that had really upset her. All Douglas would have done was asked his PA to shop for him and get everything gift-wrapped.

And Megan knew exactly what it was. The same perfume he'd given her for every present since they'd been together. Now she'd have to try and make it up to Jamie. If she could just rewind the clock, she'd open Douglas's gift and pretend she didn't care that no love had gone into the choosing of it.

When Douglas had turned up the day before they were due to travel to Scotland, she thought he'd come to discuss routes and what they'd be taking with them. She was like a child dancing round him, telling him to come and look at the map book, asking if he had his walking boots ready. Douglas had been distant and quieter than usual. Then he started saying how sorry he was and how he didn't want to hurt her. She didn't know what he was going on about, but finally his words sunk in. Finding it hard to believe what he was telling her, she asked, 'But when did you meet this woman?'

'The time scale is immaterial. The point is we've met and fallen in love.'

'Couldn't you have told me sooner; given me the chance to get over this shock before Christmas? At least I could have made other plans.' Why was she asking these things when he'd just taken a sledgehammer to her heart? He walked over and patted her shoulder as she collapsed in a chair. 'Don't touch me!'

'Really Megan, you must have known for a while that we're not right for each other. We've had a good time together, but can you really see yourself as my wife?'

'You spoke about marrying me. Why did you do that if you didn't think we were meant for each other?'

'I don't know. I suppose to keep you sweet. I can't bear whiney women.'

'So it was all a lie?'

'No, it was fine to begin with. We had good times together, didn't we?'

'But you didn't ever truly believe that we would spend the rest of our lives together?' What did it matter? He'd finished with her and she was devastated. She'd loved him, thinking that he felt the same about her. How was it she hadn't seen through his deceit? It seemed impossible that she'd been totally unaware of another woman in his life. 'I think you'd better go.'

He walked to the door, a look of relief on his face. 'One day you'll see this is for the best.'

* * *

After he'd left, Megan had cried until she was too tired to cry anymore. Now she acknowledged the thought that at least he'd had the decency to turn up himself and tell her face-to-face rather than getting his PA to send a bunch of flowers and a letter she'd composed.

She switched on the light and carefully emptied the gifts onto the table ready to share with Jamie when he returned. As she arranged them she felt them and tried to guess what they were. She'd get him to do the same. One was obviously a bottle, so she unwrapped it, and used Jamie's penknife to pull out the cork to allow the red wine to breathe. In the kitchen she polished two glasses with a cloth then searched for something nice to serve with the wine. Yet even with her newfound inventiveness she could think of nothing that would make a tasty snack.

She felt lonely without Jamie's presence. It was strange how quickly she'd got used to him being there. And she liked having him with her. She wandered into the bathroom, brushed her hair, then clipped the side back with a sparkly slide. Hoping she wasn't overdoing things, she picked out a peach lipstick. After carefully applying it she rubbed her cheeks to give them some colour.

'I'm back,' she heard Jamie calling as a gust of cold air rushed through the cottage.

His return put a smile on her face and lightened her mood.

'It's dreadful out there. What's this? A party?'

Pulling herself together, she joined

him in the living room. 'I wanted to make it up to you, for being touchy. What happened isn't your fault. So we've got a bottle of red and lots of presents to unwrap. We might find something good to eat.'

'One-track mind. I'm having the armchair if I'm the guest at your party. It's the floor for you.'

Or your lap, she thought as she sank onto the rug in front of the fire.

Jamie slopped wine into glasses before flopping into the chair. Megan noticed that he didn't even glance at the label on the bottle. That would have been the first thing Douglas would have done. She'd been in restaurants with him when he'd refused to accept the bottle he'd ordered after poring over the label. But now she was with Jamie, the heat from the fire was soothing her and she felt good.

'You've got to guess what this is,' she said, throwing a square parcel wrapped in scarlet paper towards Jamie, who missed the catch completely.

'I think it's a cut-glass decanter,' he said, picking it up from the floor.

'You'll have to unwrap it and see if you're correct. The person who gets it wrong the most has to cook our next meal.'

'Serious stakes, then.' Jamie put his glass on the floor and set his face grimly. 'Can I have another go, please? I wasn't ready.'

'You're just a big kid, aren't you?'

'Yep, that's me.'

'Go on then, have another go, as 'cut-glass decanter' doesn't count as a proper guess.'

He felt and squeezed the present. 'It's quite large and it makes a noise when you shake it.' He demonstrated by Megan's ear.

She nodded solemnly. 'Your guess is?'

'A jigsaw.' He ripped at the paper and whooped as the box came into view.

'It must be from my neighbour. She likes them too, and we often do a swap.' She looked at the top of the box. 'My goodness, all those pieces. We'll be here until well into the New Year doing that lot.' The idea didn't displease her. She risked a glance at Jamie, but he was busy helping himself to another present. 'Hey, it's my turn.'

Megan wrenched another rectangular-shaped parcel from Jamie's hands and ripped it open.

'Meg, you're not sticking to the rules. You've got to guess what it is.'

'Okay, I guess it's a box of chocolates. Black Magic. Is that close enough for you?'

'It has to be, considering you're reading from the label. What a cheat!'

Megan put the chocolates back on the table. 'We'll share those later,' she said. She noted Jamie's twinkling eyes as he watched her. Did he think anything of her, other than a port in a snow storm? What if she asked him and he said he hated her and couldn't stand being with her? What would happen then? Considering that she'd accused him of being selfish and then was so irritable about Douglas's gift, she was surprised he was still here with her. On the other hand, where could he go? She reached out and selected a gold-and-black covered packet and handed it to him. 'Your go.'

'Humm, this one's tricky. It's smartly dressed, soft and light.' He weighed it in his hand as if to prove the point. 'I think it could be hankies.'

'Who uses them? Everyone has tissues, don't they?'

'Fair enough. I give up. May I open it, please?' He waited for permission and then tore at the paper, reducing it to an untidy mess on the floor. 'I wasn't expecting this.' He gave a wide smile and held the bra and matching panties up against himself.

Horrified, Megan tried to snatch them from him. 'Not your size, bud. Give them here.' How embarrassing was that? Nevertheless, she couldn't help giggling at Jamie as he paraded up and down the living room modelling her gift. There was never a dull moment with him around. 'Whoever are they from?' She picked up the shredded mess of paper from the floor and searched for a gift tag. 'This is from my brother. That's odd, not like him at all.' Megan frowned and pursed her lips. Then she said, 'The horror. I bet he bought this for his girlfriend and then she dumped him. Thought they'd do for me.'

'Not that I'm a very good judge, and please don't go off into another fit of pique, but I'm sure these wouldn't do your figure the justice it deserves.' He half-held up his hands to his face. 'Please don't hit me.'

Megan gently pulled at his hands and blurted out, 'I don't know why I'm being mean to you. I'm really so happy to have you around, and you're such good company. I don't know how I would have managed on my own. It was all right for a couple of days while I wallowed in self-pity over the festive season, but now that there's no way out at the moment, I think I would have been scared stiff on my own — independent woman or not.'

Jamie disentangled his hands from hers and put them around her, pulling her close to his strong, reassuring chest. He said nothing, just held her; and she let herself be held, delighting in the comforting beat of his heart against her cheek.

Eventually Megan broke free, feeling light-headed. He couldn't hate her, then. 'Shall we finish opening these prezzies?' She tore off the paper of the one nearest her and revealed a bright red jumper. 'You're not the only one with a gran who knits,' she said with a smile, putting it on the bed-settee for later. 'Your go.'

Jamie picked up a parcel and started to unwrap it. 'It says 'from Dad'. I've no idea what it is, but it's quite heavy.' He pulled off the last of the paper. 'This is smart,' he said, holding up a pink towelling bathrobe with tiny red hearts splashed over it. 'And slippers to match.'

'Ooh, how lovely.' Megan stretched out her hand to touch the soft, furry fabric. Then she unfolded it with a view to wearing it straight away. Before she got that far, something dropped from it which Jamie neatly fielded.

'Another bottle of booze. Great. Look, it's champagne. Glad I caught that one.'

Dressed in her fluffy bathrobe, Megan took another gift from the table and held it out to Jamie. 'You open it. I'm so happy now that I don't mind cooking.' Desperately hoping he wouldn't ask why she'd become happy all of a sudden, Megan waited to see what the next gift would be.

'This one's from your mum,' read Jamie. 'And I think you should open it.' He handed it back to Megan.

'This is funny,' she said. 'Usually Mum and Dad give me presents from both of them. What makes it different this year?'

'Because they knew you were coming here. Perhaps they thought you'd need extra tender loving care.'

The expensive range of bath oils and

creams from her mum had Megan unscrewing the tops and smelling them and then handing them to Jamie to smell. He grinned at her. 'It would be good if we had some running water so you could use them.'

'See, she's even included a scented candle. How lovely.' Megan gave Jamie a watery look. 'I miss them,' she whispered, her chin wobbling.

'They'll be home before you know it,' encouraged Jamie, rubbing his hand up and down her arm. 'Oh look, there's another parcel left on the table.'

'You open that.'

Jamie did so. 'This is from Sandra.'

'My friend at home,' explained Megan.

Jamie nodded. 'Packet of dates, sugared almonds, crystallised ginger, nuts, packets of cookies and four — yes four — Mars bars. Meg, you have the coolest friends.'

'Yes, I do, don't I?' Megan grabbed her phone and within seconds expertly brought up a picture. 'Here,' she cried, 'this is us.' She passed the phone over for Jamie to look at.

'Hey, she looks fun. Are you in fancy dress?'

Megan snatched the device back. 'Don't be so rude. We were on our way to a party and no, it wasn't fancy dress.' She studied the picture and smiled. 'You'd never think she was the mother of a three-year-old, would you?'

Jamie shrugged. 'I've no idea what that would look like.'

'Her husband's great. He adores her and little Timmy. I wonder what they're up to now. I wish the phone would work.' Megan put away the phone and sat quietly.

'Hey, don't go moody on me,' begged Jamie, squatting down beside her. 'We'll be okay.'

'But can you promise that?'

Jamie looked at her long and hard. 'No, no I can't do that. But what I can promise is that I'll try and make sure everything's as all right as it can be. Is that enough?'

Megan looked up at him. 'None of this is your responsibility. You just happened by. I really think you should take a course in map-reading before coming this way again.'

'What about if I'm enjoying myself here?' Jamie cocked his head at her.

'With me for company I should think you're the happiest man alive,' giggled Megan, starting to feel better. 'I'll be able to visit Sandra when I get back home and she'll be hysterical hearing about my holiday with a handsome stranger.'

'Yes, don't miss that bit out, please.'

'Oh that's all right. She's used to my exaggeration. It's the actress in me.' Megan looked around the room littered with presents and Christmas wrapping. Her eyes stayed on the little frond of fir which Jamie had brought in for her. That was her best present, she decided. 'Thank you for my Christmas, Jamie.'

He grabbed her and danced her around the room until they both fell happily into the armchair.

5

Feeling awkward again, Megan disentangled herself from Jamie's arms and sat upright. 'What shall we do now?'

'Celebrate! I had a delicious Christmas dinner — turkey, stuffing, sausages, roast potatoes, carrots, sprouts . . . '

'Stop, stop!' she said, pounding her fists on his chest.

'As you haven't had much of a Christmas, this is going to be a night to remember. We're having a fancy dress party with delicious food and drink, superb decorations, a roaring fire, crackers, games and carols. I hope you can sing because I sound like a sea lion in distress.'

'Where are the crackers?' Megan asked.

'Sometimes you have to pretend.'

Megan leant back against Jamie and gazed into the fire. Wasn't that what Douglas had been doing? Pretending that he loved her when he'd already found someone else? Pretending he had work to do when really he was seeing his new woman? Pretending that he wanted to marry her? She tried unsuccessfully to stifle a sob.

'Hey, my singing's not that bad,' Jamie said, hugging her. 'Do you want to tell me about whatever it is? There's something going on here. Attractive young women don't usually hide themselves away in remote cottages for the festive season. What's up, Meg?'

Megan sniffed. 'Nobody calls me Meg.'

'I do.'

Megan had always preferred her full name, but she'd got used to Jamie calling her Meg and even begun to feel special when he did. How stupid was that?

'But if you don't like it . . . '

'I do. It's special.'

Jamie squeezed her gently. 'And so are you.'

Megan was imagining what might happen next, when a log shifted in the fire and sent sparks shooting onto the rug. She jumped up and stamped on them. 'I'm glad I hadn't put my new slippers on,' she said, studying the soles of her socks. 'What do we have to do to prepare for the party?'

'How about if I see to the food while you decorate the table. You've got to be more artistic than me. Then I'll fetch more wood, we'll change into our outfits and the party can begin. You never know who or what might turn up. The sheep will be queuing to get in.'

Megan went to the window and peered out. 'Nobody else will get here, I'm pretty sure about that. Not even very determined carol singers. It's snowing heavily again. Just how much longer is this going to go on for?' She wasn't sure how she felt. It would be so lovely to go home and enjoy all the comforts, but she didn't want her time with Jamie to end. She sensed that he wouldn't have given her a second look if they'd met in normal circumstances.

'I'll put the champagne out to chill.'

Jamie opened the door and jammed the bottle down into the snow. 'There are advantages to this dreadful weather. And that's not the only one.'

Seeing the look he gave her, she knew exactly what he meant. Instead of always planning for the future, she must make the most of the present, and right now she was trapped in a cottage with Jamie, the funniest and kindest man she'd ever met. He was a live wire, always laughing, not a hint of pretension about him. There had been several occasions when Jamie could have snapped at her or even sulked, but he didn't do that. He simply bounced back with good humour and sparkling banter.

Douglas was attractive in a well-groomed sort of way and she'd thought him kind until he'd told her he was leaving and said the cruellest things. His new girlfriend was welcome to him. Unexpectedly Megan realised that was the first time she'd had that thought. Until now she'd imagined she'd give anything to have Douglas back in her life. But if he turned up at the door now, having struggled through the snow to find her, she was almost certain she'd turn him away. The thought made her feel as though a huge weight had been lifted from her shoulders.

The clattering of pots in the kitchen reminded her that she should be getting on with her task. She wondered what she could use to make decorations. Then she set to work, smoothing out the torn and crumpled wrapping paper, using the kitchen scissors to cut it into strips and sticking it together with eyelash adhesive to make paper chains which she draped round the room. She tugged the dining table away from the wall and pulled out the leaves. Placing the fragrant candle her mum had given her in the centre of the table, she looked around for inspiration. Seeing Jamie's Christmas tree, she broke off small bits of fir twig wrapped it round into a circle and she had the perfect napkin holder. For napkins she used tissues.

She was sitting thinking of how else to decorate the table when Jamie wandered in. 'How's it going? Nice paperchains! Any ideas for fancy dress?'

'Not really. What about you?'

'It's not easy, is it?' Jamie said, frowning.

'No, we might have to give it a miss. I could dress up in my new bathrobe and slippers. How's the Christmas dinner coming along?'

'Good. I think you'll be quite impressed by my culinary skills. I'm just going to nip out and get the wood. Will you lay the table? We're going to need the best silver, and don't forget the champagne glasses.'

Megan sorted through the mismatched cutlery and tried to find some that didn't look too bad together. Then she remembered the ribbon which had adorned Sandra's gift. She cut it in two and tied it into bows round the stems of two very ordinary wine glasses. She found two eggcups, piled sugared almonds into them and placed them at each setting. Looking at the table, she burst out laughing. It was so different from last Christmas, which she'd spent at Douglas's apartment. Everything had been perfect — shining, sparkling perfection. She'd been impressed with the thought and care that he'd put into the decorations with the silver-and-purple colour scheme. Now she knew the truth. He'd paid someone to put on the show for her.

There was a banging and Jamie called, 'Can you open the door please? I've got my hands full.' She leapt up to help.

Having placed the box on the hearth, he studied his hand. 'I've got a splinter.'

'You should have worn gloves, handling those split logs. Let me see.' She held his hand and tried to concentrate. 'Ooh, it's nasty. We need a needle.'

'Just kiss it better, Meg,' he said squeezing her hand.

'Don't be childish. That won't help.' She swiped his hand away. 'That's not burning I can smell, is it?'

With Jamie safely back in the kitchen she was able to think about her situation. She was sharing a cottage with a man she knew nothing about, but whom she felt completely at home with. She'd never experienced being her carefree self with Douglas. She'd always had to try hard to be more than she was, to impress him and his acquaintances. The reality was she'd never truly been relaxed with him. She tried to picture him here now in the cottage with her. He'd be moaning and complaining and telling her it was all her fault.

'We wish you a merry Christmas, we wish you a merry Christmas, we wish you a merry Christmas and a happy new year' boomed out from the kitchen.

Megan grinned. Jamie had been right, he really was a terrible singer. 'Is the food ready yet?' she called. 'I'm starving.'

'Just a few minutes to go,' came the

reply. 'Is the fire okay?'

Megan threw a couple more logs on and encouraged it with the poker. The temperature in the room increased. 'I think I've got the hang of this fire now,' she shouted through to Jamie.

'Hold that thought . . . for next time.'

Next time, thought Megan. *I hope there won't be a next time*. Not that she wasn't enjoying herself now, but she never wanted a repeat of the misery she'd endured when she'd come here on Christmas Eve.

'Ta da . . . ' Jamie entered the room bearing two plates which he held aloft.

Megan sucked in a breath and blinked hard. 'What are you up to?' she gasped.

'Don't you like it?' Jamie swaggered around the room, still carrying the plates. 'You said fancy dress.'

'No, I didn't. *You* said fancy dress.'

'There you are then. I win the prize, as you haven't even tried to enter the competition with a costume.'

'Oh, Jamie, you're so funny. I love your outfit.'

'I suppose you should have worn it, but it's sooo not your colour.' Jamie, wearing the undies Megan's brother had given her over his trousers, placed a plate in front of Megan and the other one beside her. 'Bon appétit, madame,' he said with a bow.

'I set your place over the other side of the table,' protested Megan, put out that her arrangements were being altered.

'All the way over there?' Jamie put a hand to his eyebrows as if scanning a distant horizon. 'How will we pull the crackers?'

'But you said we didn't have . . . ' Then she caught his expression and broke off, laughing again. He really was excellent company and he seemed to know when to be light-hearted and when to be serious. She merely raised her eyebrows and ignored him. She poked her knife around the plate. 'And this is?'

'That good old-fashioned English Christmas starter, Spam fritters, of course,' he smiled, forking some into his mouth and chewing hard. 'Delicious.'

Megan cut off a small corner and put it into her mouth. 'Mmm, not bad. Not bad at all.'

When Jamie's plate was empty, he excused himself and disappeared into the kitchen for the main course. Gazing around the festive room, Megan thought what a brilliant transformation had taken place. Those paper chains and the decorated table made such a difference. When she'd finished her first course, she screwed a length of leftover wrapping paper into a spill and, taking a light from the fire, lit the candle. There was just enough flickering light from it and the fire to create a softened atmosphere. Then she opened the cupboard next to the settee and took out the small radio, tuning it to a music station. She hummed along, wondering why she hadn't used it much before.

'Has there been a power cut as well?' asked Jamie, coming in from the kitchen.

'I thought this would give a more

Christmassy feel,' muttered Megan, only just realising that her action could have been misconstrued. She ticked herself off and then asked, 'Shall I turn the light back on? It is a bit dark, isn't it?'

'My Christmas dinner was made to be eaten in the dark,' quipped Jamie, depositing a large plate at each of their places. 'Dîner à la maison.'

'You've worked really hard, Jamie,' said Megan. 'I never expected to have salmon for dinner.'

'Don't forget the tinned potatoes and spinach.' They exchanged a smile, recognising that together they'd created an evening worthy of the term 'celebration'.

Abruptly, Megan clattered her knife and fork onto her plate and rushed outside.

'Hey, Meg, are you okay?' Jamie jumped up and followed her. 'My cooking can't be that bad. What's up? Are you ill?'

With the front door wide open

Megan was outlined by the frame. She turned to him. 'It's snowing again.'

'You left my excellent cuisine for a weather forecast?' He stared at her open-mouthed.

'No, I came for this.' She held up the bottle of champagne. Jamie ushered her inside and quickly slammed the front door. Back at the table they tucked in, hardly talking; and very soon, with empty plates and a near-empty bottle, Megan and Jamie reclined in their chairs.

'Pudding?'

'Later, please,' said Megan. 'Ooh, listen to that music.'

'Would you like to dance?' Jamie was on his feet with his arm extended towards her.

Giggling, Megan struggled to her feet and took his hand. 'I love salsa, don't you?'

Looking puzzled, Jamie said, 'Salsa, as in sauce, do you mean?'

Sighing dramatically, Megan explained, 'Salsa is a dance. It is also a sauce, you're right, but I meant that I love salsa dancing.' When she saw him grinning she realised he'd been teasing her.

'Right, I've seen people doing it, but . . . ' frowned Jamie, swirling her round and executing movements that no self-respecting dancer would have put up with.

Megan shrugged and gave in as she followed his lumbering movements. At length they both staggered to a halt as the music stopped and the programme turned to a more serious news report. They returned to the table and finished the champagne.

'Happy Christmas, Meg,' toasted Jamie. 'I hope you've enjoyed yourself.'

Dreamily, Megan nodded her head, smiling broadly. 'I've had a great time. Thank you.'

Jamie moved his chair nearer to her and put his hand on hers. *Oh dear, please don't let things be spoilt now*, begged Megan to herself. When, *if*, Jamie wanted things to hot up between them, she didn't want it under these circumstances. She wanted to be stone-cold sober and away from this place which still reminded her of Christmas lost, rather than Christmas past. Gently she wriggled her fingers free from his. 'More wood, Jamie — look, the fire's nearly had it. It'll be freezing later.'

'Okay,' he said, bounding up and taking the box outside.

'Put your jacket on,' yelled Megan. 'And don't forget your gloves.' He was outside by then. Why should she worry? *Yes*, she asked herself, *why are you mothering him?* While she waited for his return, Megan snuffed out the candle, breathing in its fragrance and thinking of her own mother again. Over the past few days she'd longed to be with her family in Spain, but now she wasn't sure she'd rush out to join them. She put the main light on and turned the radio off. It was then that she heard a bellow from outside.

6

Without a thought for any danger which might be lurking out there, Megan rushed to discover what was going on. Halfway to the wood stack she could make out a dark shape on the ground.

'Jamie, is that you?'

'Yes,' he moaned.

'What happened?' she said, kneeling down by him.

'I slipped. Probably something to do with the path being so icy now. I've really hurt my ankle. It's agony. I've lost my glasses; can you see them anywhere?'

Megan hunted round and after several minutes heard a snap under her foot. 'I'm so sorry, Jamie,' she said picking up the spectacles. 'I've broken them.'

'It's the least of my worries. Will you

just shove them in your pocket?'

'You can't stay here, it's freezing. Let me help you up.' Megan struggled to get Jamie to his feet. 'Right, put your arm round my shoulders and don't put any weight on your foot.'

Jamie limped to the cottage, supported by Megan, and collapsed in the chair. 'How thick am I? I'm not going to be much use now. I didn't even manage to get the wood.'

'Don't worry. I'll go and fetch it and then there's nothing else to do this evening.' Tiredness hit her. It had been a busy day and Jamie wasn't a small man. Supporting him back to the cottage had been the last straw.

'Don't forget your coat and gloves; it's bitter out there,' Jamie said kindly.

Walking along the little path, she realised how slippery it had become, and in spite of treading carefully soon lost her balance and was on the ground. Finding that she wasn't hurt at all, she picked herself up and continued with her task. Soon she was back in the snug living room. Having stacked the wood by the fire and put another couple of logs on, she considered what she should do about Jamie's ankle.

'Any ideas about treatment?' she asked him.

'Ice pack?' he suggested.

'Right.' Back outside she piled snow into a plastic bag and took it in. 'I think you should have your foot up. If I get one of the hard-backed chairs and put a cushion on it you can rest your foot on that.'

With Jamie settled, she took a look at his ankle. Already there was vivid purple swelling. 'That looks painful.'

'It is.' Jamie grimaced.

'I'm going to put the snow pack in Gran's jumper and put it against your ankle, then I'm going to hunt for pain-killers.' She didn't have a clue about first aid, but realised there wasn't a lot they could do. It was probably just a case of plenty of rest, which wouldn't be difficult as there was so little to do here. They were hardly going to go jogging or trekking over the mountains. Finding a packet of painkillers in her toilet bag, she hurried back to Jamie, who was fidgeting.

'What's up now?' she asked.

'You broke my glasses. How will I manage?'

Megan had completely forgotten about the damaged spectacles and hurriedly fetched them from her coat pocket. 'They're not as bad as I thought. It's just one of the arms that's snapped off. I'm sure I can fix it.'

'Yeah, right, and I can run a marathon.'

Megan fetched her toilet bag. 'Look, I've got these big plasters. If I wrap one round like this they're as good as new. Well, not quite.' She leant over Jamie and perched the spectacles perilously on his nose.

'Thanks, Meg, they're perfect.'

It wasn't long before Jamie was groaning again.

'What is it, Jamie?'

'I won't be able to drive. Suppose it

thawed tomorrow. You'll go home and leave me and I'll be stuck here, not able to move.'

'Don't be ridiculous. It's not going to thaw tomorrow.'

'That's not nice or funny.'

'Okay, I'll try again. Don't be ridiculous. I wouldn't dream of leaving you to fend for yourself.' She grinned at him. 'I need to ask you something. Do you always get flu and never colds?'

'Very funny. Look, my ankle's getting worse.'

Megan examined it again. It had ballooned since she'd last looked. 'Do you think we should strap it up or something?'

'I think your tender loving care will do the trick. If I could just have something to take those painkillers with I'll be fine.'

Once again Megan had to go outside to get snow to melt. She took her time to enjoy the still, moonlit night. Really, if the circumstances were different, it would be magical. Then she remembered that Jamie was waiting.

Jamie dozed in the chair while she washed and wiped up. Everything was so much harder in this situation. It was late and she was feeling shattered, but she'd have to let Jamie have the bed and she'd sleep in the armchair. She didn't want the possibility of kicking him in the night.

'Jamie,' she whispered, 'time for bed.'

'Really?' he asked dozily.

'Let me help you, then you can have the bed to yourself.' She left him at the entrance to the bathroom and got the bed-settee ready, then waited to help him back. Once he was safely tucked in she wiped her face and did her best to clean her teeth, then tried to get comfortable in the chair.

'Meg?'

'Yes, what is it?' she snapped. Why did he have to go and spoil their evening by being so clumsy?

'There's no point you trying to sleep in the chair. I know how uncomfortable it is. It won't hurt if you join me here. We can put a cushion to protect my ankle.'

'I'm not risking it. The sooner you are up and about the better.'

'Please, Meg, I miss you.'

'Go to sleep.'

Just as she was about to doze off, Jamie's voice made her jump. 'Meg, I can't sleep. My ankle's throbbing; it's awful.'

'Jamie, what do you expect me to do about it? I've done everything I can in the circumstances. Go to sleep. It's the best healer.' She punched the cushion she was using as a pillow and closed her eyes. What she would give to be in her own home. She imagined standing under the shower with the steam filling her bathroom . . .

'Meg? Did you remember to put the milk bottles out?'

'It's not funny, Jamie.' Her eyes drooping, she imagined her mum's rhubarb crumble covered in thick cream, a treacle tart with crumbly pastry . . .

'Meg, are you awake? The snow's melting.'

'That's ludicrous. How would you

know, lying there in your cosy bed? And anyway, it's hardly going to start melting in the middle of the night when the temperature's well below zero. Please go to sleep.'

'I mean it, the snow's melting. The water's leaking out of the plastic bag.'

'Right.' Megan's patience was waning. She retrieved the bag and emptied it into the kitchen sink. 'There's no point you having another. By the morning it will have melted all over the bed.'

'Will you join me now? I'm freezing. Probably the shock.'

'For goodness sake. For the last time, go to sleep. I'm wrecked and that bubbly has given me a headache. I just need a good night.'

'Sorry, Meg. Night night.'

Once again she closed her eyes. She thought of her centrally heated bedroom, her bed with its comfortable mattress, the . . .

'Meg, are you asleep? It was a lovely evening, wasn't it?'

Jamie sounded so pitiful she couldn't

help laughing. 'You're pathetic,' she spluttered.

'But you like me.'

'Yes, I like you. Good job too, as we're probably stuck here together for some time to come.'

'Come to bed, please,' he pleaded. 'Neither of us will sleep if we're cold. It's silly. We'll be useless tomorrow.'

'It won't make much difference to you then, will it?' she asked unkindly. The springs of the armchair were digging into her back and there was no way she would get comfortable. She got up and threw some more logs onto the fire before creeping over to the bed, snuggling down into Jamie's empty sleeping bag and gently settling beside him.

'Happy now you've got what you wanted?' she asked.

'Very happy. It's time for you to have some TLC now,' Jamie whispered. 'Tell me exactly where your head aches and I'll soon make you feel better.'

'Just here,' she said touching her

forehead. 'Jamie,' she began, 'if you could choose a place to go for a holiday, where would you go?'

'Umm, that's a tough one. I'd probably choose a deserted house in the depths of Scotland with no food, but excellent company. And what about you?'

Megan turned on her back and stared at the dark ceiling. 'Barbados appeals right now. I nearly went, you know.'

'Tell me,' whispered Jamie, stroking her forehead.

'A couple of years ago I'd almost booked it up with a friend when I got a part in the local theatre. I was so excited about that. If I'd known the play was going to fold in a couple of days I'd have been on those warm foreign beaches.'

'I know what you mean about the warmth, but I'm not too good in extremes of temperature.'

'I'd noticed,' muttered Megan. 'Okay, okay, I'm sorry. I know you're in pain. Actually, when I was younger it was often difficult to get away as we had a dog. He hated the kennels and we felt really mean when he had to go in there when a family crisis took us down to Devon.'

'We had a dog.'

'Ours was called Rover — how original was that? What about yours?'

'Dog,' said Jamie.

'Yes, what was your dog called?' said Megan slowly as if talking to a small child.

'Dog. That's it. His name was Dog,' explained Jamie, a light bubble of a smile in his voice.

Megan shook with laughter as she said, 'Trust you. I bet you thought of that name, didn't you?' She felt Jamie's head nod against hers. 'What other pets have you had? I had rats. They are the cutest animals. And so intelligent.'

'Eurgh! How could you? We had guinea pigs.'

'Called?' enquired Megan

'Do I have to say? I suppose you'll laugh. They were Bubble and Squeak.'

'Wouldn't you just love some bubble

and squeak with cold chicken and baked beans? Or vanilla ice-cream with deep, rich, hot chocolate sauce?'

'Torture. Let's change the subject. Okay, looks like we're playing the favourites game.' Jamie resumed stroking her forehead.

'Are we?' Megan asked.

'You started it. What's your favourite type of car?'

'I love VW camper vans and I wouldn't say no to a Peugot 307 convertible. And you?'

'I like blue ones.'

'Oh, Jamie, you're impossible.'

'Favourite way to spend Sunday morning?'

'On a cold winter's day, going for a lovely walk in the snow followed by breakfast in a café with the windows steaming up and everyone being friendly and cheerful. On a hot day, taking a good book to read by the river, feeding the ducks and having a picnic.' Thinking back, she and Douglas hadn't done either of those two things. Most Sundays they'd entertained or been entertained in smart, expensive restaurants where it didn't matter what the weather was like outside. 'What about you?'

'Same as you,' Jamie said sleepily.

With Jamie's hand still caressing her forehead, Megan fell into a deep sleep full of dreams of strange Christmas meals and useless gifts.

* * *

Jamie's head was whirling as it had been ever since he'd met the enchanting occupant of this cottage. His plan for a few relaxing, recharging days had gone awry. He was used to being awake in the middle of the night and stirring up ideas in his mind. It seemed that work was his whole life, and it was so important at this vital juncture that he felt guilty for lounging around doing nothing towards the goals he'd set himself.

Painfully slipping from the bed, not wanting to disturb Meg, Jamie hobbled around the room until he located his penknife and then edged towards the fire. He threw on a couple of logs, selected a small piece of wood from the pile and slumped against the armchair. As he whittled away at the wood, his mind took over and he thought out the next stage of his work. He should be in touch with his team, but at the moment that wasn't possible. Therefore he should do the next best thing, which was to write down any ideas that occurred to him and wait until he was back in Edinburgh in a few days. Then he remembered that his notebooks were back in the car and cursed the fact that he wouldn't be able to get them because of his unfortunate accident. Knowing that he couldn't do more than he was doing already, he continued with his carving until fatigue overtook him. He replaced the penknife where he'd found it and tucked the fashioned piece of wood into his pocket. Then he limped back into the bed, pulling the covers around him.

7

Megan was woken by the cold surrounding her body. Snapping open her eyes, she saw that Jamie had enveloped himself in the covers and had left her exposed to the elements, after she'd half-squirmed out of the sleeping bag. A glance at the fireplace told her the fire had gone out. Jamie snored lightly, but didn't stir enough to be awake. She'd best leave him to sleep while she sorted out the fire and brought in more snow for tea. Unless the water had forced its way along the pipes. A quick turn of the tap in the bathroom told her that it hadn't. She used the damp tissues once more, and then cleaned her teeth as best she could. As she pulled a brush through her tangled hair, she thought about their absurd situation.

Once outside, it was clear that the thaw was nowhere near arriving. Frost sparkled on the trees and an eerie silence pervaded the air. For the first time since coming here, Megan was afraid. What if they never got out? No one had missed them so far, it seemed. They'd be skeletons draped over a game of Monopoly before anyone came to rescue them. She bent to shovel snow into the washing-up bowl and returned to the cottage.

Soon the kettle was coming to the boil and a couple of pans were full of icy water awaiting their turn to be heated later on.

'Tea up, Jamie,' she called, bending to put his mug on the floor by the bed.

He replied with a grunt. She sipped the weak tea, enjoying the sensation of the hot liquid coursing through her. When Megan had drained the mug, she called, 'Come on, Jamie, tea up. It's getting cold.' There was still no answer.

Megan hung the jumper her gran had knitted on the back of one of the dining chairs, hoping it would soon dry out as she was still freezing. Now that she felt properly awake, she disappeared outside again to bring in more wood. Jamie wouldn't be any help today. *Poor thing*, she thought, *I've been terribly mean to him. He must be in agony.* The fire was blazing once again, but Jamie still didn't stir.

It was getting on for lunchtime when another growl came from the bed. Megan looked up from her book. 'Feeling better?'

'Not really. I could do with some tea, though. Any chance of a cuppa?'

Megan pointed to the still-full mug on the floor by him.

'Right. Thanks.' He lifted it to his lips and took a gulp. 'Yuk, what's this? It's cold.'

'It wasn't cold when I put it there,' retorted Megan. Muttering, she put the kettle on again and brewed more tea. She was glad to have some herself, but was conscious that she had used up all their supplies of tea with these last mugs.

'Thank you,' smiled Jamie. 'I don't

mean to be a pain.'

Megan shrugged. 'It's all right. You couldn't help it. When you've finished your tea, I'll help you to the bathroom.'

'You've got a good fire going there,' observed Jamie, gesturing with the mug which spilt over the bed.

Jumping up, Megan dabbed at it with her sleeve. 'You'd better get up now. You're a complete disaster area.'

Meekly, Jamie did as he was told. Later, with the bed made and everything straightened in the room, Megan relaxed. She'd never thought of herself as a tidy person, but the disorder Jamie brought unnerved her. He was like a St Bernard dog, but more demanding now he wasn't feeling good.

Douglas had often complained about her untidiness and lack of planning, but when she thought of his flat what had once seemed stylish and minimalist now seemed cold and unfriendly. Douglas was always organised and there had never been any room for spontaneity. She could see that being with Jamie would be spontaneous and, what had been missing from her relationship with Douglas, fun.

'You'd better have some more pain-killers,' said Megan, handing over two tablets.

'Ta. Can I have a drink to get them down, please?' Jamie wriggled on the bed, adjusting the pillows.

And just what did your last servant die of? Aloud, Megan said, 'I'll get it.'

He called after her, 'Is it lunchtime yet?'

Megan swallowed down yet another biting response as she handed him a cup of water. 'Lunch will have to be the pudding you made yesterday.'

Jamie pulled a face. 'Bagsy you taste first.' He put the tablets into his mouth and made a great performance of swigging them down.

'Remind me what this is again,' asked Megan, pushing the contents of the dish around.

'It's Sandra's cookies crushed with nuts and slices of crystallised ginger.

The topping's pieces of Mars bar. Can I have custard with mine?'

'Jamie have you had a complete personality change, or perhaps that should be *bypass*? I've been running in and out of the cottage, stoking the fire and waiting on you while you've reclined like some nabob. It's a pity you've hurt your ankle, but please don't treat me like your slave.' Megan could feel a heat in her face that wasn't the result of the fire. She watched him taking in what she'd said. Had she gone too far? He may run off and she'd be on her own. Ha! He couldn't, could he? He'd have to stay.

Slowly Jamie eased himself off the bed and took her hand. 'Meg, I should have been more thoughtful. My ankle hurts like anything, but that's no reason to be insensitive to you.'

Megan was taken aback. This was the old Jamie. Men could be pretty dire when they were under the weather, and his ankle certainly was badly bruised and swollen. They sat holding hands until Megan's composure returned.

'You're right,' she said with a smile, drawing his hand gently down her cheek, 'it would be better with custard. I'll go and open the tin.'

Having made friends again, they sat on the floor with the Monopoly board in front of them. Jamie had far more property and money than Megan, but she didn't care; she'd never been competitive with games.

'Rent!' yelled Jamie, 'Let's see, that's . . . ' Megan smiled as she watched him adding up what she owed him. However, she also knew that he was hiding a lot of pain and discomfort from her. The winces were silent now since her outburst, but his eyes and the occasional twist of his mouth told her he was suffering. Since Jamie's arrival at the cottage, Megan had let him take charge until today when he'd been unable to. She must take it upon herself to get them rescued, as she was sure Jamie's ankle needed more attention than she knew how to give it.

'Bad luck. Fancy another game?' asked Jamie, fanning himself ostentatiously with his wad of winnings.

'I'll let you quit while you're ahead,' said Megan, stretching and looking around the room. 'I suppose we could do the jigsaw.'

'Okay. But jigsaws are the one thing I'm not good at.'

Megan made a face at him.

'All right, there are one or two other things I'm not good at as well as jigsaws, but I'm not admitting to all my failings right now. I can't see us finishing it, but let's make a start,' said Jamie. 'We can put it on the table.'

'That means we'll have to pull the leaves out and it'll take up most of the room. How about the floor?' Megan was about to empty the tiny pieces out of the box when she looked over at Jamie. 'Change of plan,' she said. 'You'd only step on it and knock it for six. What we need is a hard surface we can move about. Is my suitcase any good, do you think?'

Jamie shuffled over and thumped it with his balled fist. 'Nope, it's too soft. Hang on.'

Megan heard him banging about in the kitchen. 'What're you doing? If you've found more chocolate biscuits, you'd better share.'

Grinning, Jamie clattered a large tray down in front of her. 'Clever or what?'

'Well done. I'll save the praise for when you've done the outside bits of this picture.'

'Your neighbour's obviously got a sense of humour,' grimaced Jamie. 'A sweltering beach scene and several thousand tiny pieces.'

Megan giggled. 'Here, this is a corner piece. You can put that in.' She handed over the small section and watched while Jamie dithered over which corner to insert it in.

They worked together and managed to get one side done. 'This is fun,' said Jamie. 'I don't think I've done a jigsaw since I was a kid.'

But Megan was bored now and on

the verge of giving up. Jamie leaned across her to grab a piece of blue. 'Sky,' he said, lifting it up like a prize. Then he lost his balance and fell into Megan's shoulder. She wasn't prepared for the delightful effect that his closeness had on her. He gazed at her, his eyes for once serious.

'I'm not going to apologise,' he murmured. Abruptly, he righted himself and delved into the box for another piece. 'We're doing well,' he observed, apparently concentrating on the picture on the lid of the box.

With renewed enthusiasm Megan hunted through the carton for more edge pieces, and it was some time later when Jamie yawned that she suggested they should stop for the day.

'Let me put it somewhere safe,' she said, taking the tray and carefully sliding it under the bed-settee. 'Why don't you get back on the bed and prop your leg up on this pillow. I'll go and see what there is for our next meal. Supplies are going down rather.'

Jamie hopped onto the bed and Megan made him as comfortable as possible. 'Just remembered these,' she said, dragging the cellophane cover off the box of chocolates. 'Here, help yourself. Don't forget I like the caramel and nut ones.'

'I go for the soft centres myself,' said Jamie, popping a couple into his mouth before leaning back on the pillows and closing his eyes.

'What's that?' Megan asked, suddenly alert again.

'What? What can you hear? Has someone come to rescue us?'

'No, it's a scratching noise. There's something in the cottage. Maybe a mouse.' Megan searched round the room.

Jamie asked, 'You don't mind mice, do you?'

'Don't be daft, course not. Why, do you?' Megan was surprised at his question.

'They stir up bad memories in me.' He curled himself up, shivering slightly.

'I think the noise was coming from

over here. Ah ha. There's a little hole in the skirting board; I expect it's scurried back there. Never mind.' Megan made her way to the kitchen.

'You're not going to leave it there, are you?'

'Why not? It's not doing us any harm. It's hardly going to eat our supplies. We haven't got anything much.'

'But I won't be able to sleep now,' Jamie complained. 'I think we . . . you should catch it and put it out of the cottage.'

'Outside, in the cold? No way. Anyway, it's been here ever since you have. The situation is no different.'

Jamie sighed. 'I know and I don't want it to suffer. But there's no way I can relax if I'm continually listening out for its scrabbling.'

'Right, I'll catch it.' Megan planned to release it in the wood shed. She couldn't bear to think of it outside in the snow, and it had probably lived in the cottage for ages anyway. She went into the kitchen to look for a container to turn into a mouse trap. Then all that was needed was something to tempt it with. She decided to try Christmas cake crumbs as bait, but wasn't quite sure how this was going to work. She'd have to watch for the mouse to go into the trap and somehow be quick enough to shut it in there. She set a plastic container with the cake crumbs by the mouse hole and hoped that would satisfy Jamie for the time being.

'There you are. As soon as I hear it's in the box I'll bung the lid on and take it outside. I'll sit and read for a bit.'

* * *

Jamie stretched out on the bed and Megan tried to concentrate on her book. She waited until Jamie's slow, even breathing told her he was asleep before donning all her thick clothes once again and letting herself quietly out of the cottage. The board game had taken most of the afternoon and the sky was inky black. In her pocket was her mobile phone which she hoped she could use if she made her way further down the winding road.

Trudging on, she thought about Jamie. Despite their falling-out last night and today, she was growing really fond of him. Dare she let herself feel more deeply for him? What if he turned out to be as bad as Douglas? She didn't trust herself with her judgement of men anymore and she didn't want to get hurt again. It would be more than she could bear. Then a small voice of reason whispered to her that she didn't even know if Jamie fancied her.

Her thoughts had caused her to wander randomly along the road and she panicked as she realised she was lost. Running round in circles didn't help one bit, but it made her feel less chilled. And then she was rewarded as she glimpsed the roof of Jamie's car. Now she knew where she was and she pulled out her phone to check if the signal had returned.

With a sinking heart she looked at

the screen. There was still no signal. She'd try going further down the road, or would it be better to go up to a higher point? She knew nothing about signals or where masts might be positioned. Probably not out in the wilds at all. Deciding that going to high ground was the best option, she started plodding up the road. It was heavy going as the snow was deep, and each step an effort. It was also eerie with the strange light from the snow and the silence. She stopped and shivered. Turning quickly, she made sure no one was following her. *Don't be ludicrous*, she told herself. *There won't be another fool out tonight*. Having made a bit of headway, she checked her phone again. Still nothing. She felt like flinging it in the snow, but instead shoved it into her pocket and headed back.

She walked for what seemed like ages, hoping Jamie's car would soon appear, but there was no sign of it. Looking around, she longed to catch sight of the cottage just as Jamie had done that first night. If only she could spot a light or a flume of smoke from the chimney. And then she heard it.

'Hallooo . . . Hallooo . . . Meg . . . Meg . . . '

'Jamie, Jamie,' Megan shrieked, turning right and running towards the sound of Jamie's voice. Seconds later she landed in a pile of deep snow. Laughing and crying, she stumbled back to her feet and in seconds was in Jamie's arms, sobbing.

'Hey there, Meg, it's okay. You're safe. Come on, let's get you inside.' Gently taking her hand, he hobbled back into the cottage and led her to the fire. 'Let's take these wet things off.'

Megan let Jamie take control. He told her she wasn't to leave the comfort of the fire and he would make a hot drink.

After much limping and wincing, they settled on the floor. She took a sip of the drink, then looked inside the mug. 'What is this?' Megan knew they'd already used the last of the tea.

'Hot water. Have a chocolate to go with it.' He passed her the box and she saw that he hadn't touched her favourites. 'I woke up and you weren't here. I thought you were so hacked off with me you'd left. Then I reasoned you'd know how useless I am and wouldn't abandon me. You were gone ages. I was scared you'd been trapped in a snowdrift or were lying injured somewhere.'

'I was just lost. I shouldn't have gone off without telling you, but I was anxious about your leg. I thought I might get a signal and be able to phone for help.'

'I'm loads better. Didn't you see me hobbling earlier?'

'What does your ankle look like now?'

Jamie pulled up the leg of his jeans. 'I can't wear my socks, they're too tight.'

'What did you wear when you came out in the snow?'

'Nothing. It would have taken ages to get the wellies on so I didn't bother.'

They both gazed at his foot.

'Your ankle still looks awful, but I don't think it's any worse than it was.' She felt relieved.

'No, it's getting better. The snow might have done it some good. I'll be running round tomorrow. I'll look after you then. You deserve it after everything you've done for me.' He took her hand.

'You are so sweet and kind. And I've been so grumpy and miserable. I'm sorry.'

'You have been enduring this for slightly longer than me. Are you going to tell me why you came here on your own for Christmas?' He looked at her quizzically.

'Oh, I don't know; it's not a great story.' She wasn't sure she wanted to talk about it yet.

'Is it one about a broken heart?'

'Yes.' Maybe it wouldn't hurt to tell Jamie. She'd have to tell all her family and friends when she got home.

Jamie held her hand to his lips and kissed it before reaching for her face. As their lips drew close he pulled back. 'No, that's not fair. We mustn't. I'm not going to take advantage of you while you're vulnerable.'

Megan didn't feel vulnerable. All she knew was that she felt an intense attraction to this man with his dark hair, stubble, inviting eyes and an endearing ability to make her laugh. Jamie settled back with his arm lightly round her shoulders.

'It's time we knew something about each other. You first?' he asked.

Megan took a deep breath. 'Okay. His name's Douglas. He's an advertising executive and owns the firm which did that yoghurt TV advert. There was a big party in a swish London hotel and that was where we met. We fell in love, simple as that. At least, that's what I did. I'm not so sure what his feelings were. We've . . . I mean we'd been together about eighteen months, and this Christmas we opted to get away from it all on our own so we booked this cottage. Thinking back now it was more my thing than his; he just went along with it. I suppose because he had other things on his mind.

'Another woman?'

'Yep. When I found out the day before we were due to come here, I knew I couldn't face Christmas with friends or family. I just wanted to get away from everything, so I came here anyway. It wasn't such a great idea.'

'No?'

'Okay, Jamie, it wasn't a great idea until you came along.'

'That's better!' He stroked her hand. 'Is it definitely over?'

'I don't know. If he asked me to go back with him, what would I do? It's difficult. I loved him so much. I imagined us spending the whole of our lives together. It sounds soppy, but he was the only person I've ever truly loved.'

'It's not soppy. I know exactly what you mean. Shake me and you'll hear I too have a broken heart. But in my case we both wanted to be together. We didn't fall out, and neither of us found someone else. We loved each other with a passion. If you look in the side pocket of my bag there's a photo.'

Megan was intrigued. She fetched the crumpled photo and rejoined Jamie. The picture was of a beautiful girl with dark hair and a huge smile.

'She's gorgeous. What happened?'

Jamie smoothed out the photo. 'She's alive and well and I hope she's happy in her marriage. We met when I was travelling. I'm not greedy, but I had two gap years before uni. I had the best time and when I met Tami everything seemed to fall into place. That wasn't her proper name, but it's what I always called her. Meeting her was like a million Christmases all come at once. Except that her family don't celebrate Christmas. That was the problem — I was of the wrong religion. We tried hard to get her family to accept me, but it wasn't to be. And she wasn't prepared to disobey her parents. Leaving her to come back to Scotland was the worse thing that's ever happened in my life.'

'That's tragic.' Megan had been so wrapped up in her own miserable loss she'd forgotten that nearly everyone had some sad tale. She could see that Jamie was miles away and stayed quiet until he was ready to come back to her.

Jamie pictured Tami's smile and heard her laugh. It was torture remembering her and their love for each other. If things had been different they could have been married and happily settled now. He would have moved to her country. He would have done anything for her. But here he was unexpectedly with another beautiful, clever, funny, caring girl and his feelings for her were surprising. It hadn't been possible to move on from Tami, but now maybe he was ready. Feeling Megan's eyes on him he said, 'There are things you just have to accept. I'm happy enough.'

'But you do think about her?'

'A million times a day.'

8

Now that Megan knew Jamie's past, she kicked herself for being such a romantic fool as to imagine that they might, in time, get close when they got back to the real world. All he wanted was food, shelter and companionship. Right, well she'd make sure that was all there was on the agenda. Although the food was fast depleting and she was fed up with traipsing out into the freezing cold to chop and collect wood.

'Hey, Meg, what do you think?' Jamie's cheeky grin shook her out of her private thoughts.

'What? Oh, going out are you? Is it raining?' Megan looked at the ancient, dusty and probably holey umbrella that Jamie was holding.

'A crutch,' he said, waving it in front of her.

'Then stop using it as an offensive

weapon,' Megan scolded as she ducked.

Jamie showed off by walking around the room, his steps getting quicker and quicker.

'Be careful. You don't want to . . . ' It was too late, he'd already fallen. To his credit, he tried to laugh it off, but Megan could see he'd landed heavily again on his injured ankle and his spectacles had toppled to the floor. She sighed as she went to help him. 'Will you just behave? I can't keep picking you up.'

'Just leave me here for a few secs. I'll be all right, I promise. Try not to tread on my glasses again.' Jamie breathed heavily and closed his eyes.

Megan took him at his word, thinking it was something to do with male pride, and wandered into the kitchen where she stacked the few tins and packets which were left. Plucking up something from the worktop, she returned to Jamie, who was once again ensconced in the armchair.

'Here, want to share?' She held out

both hands to him, her fingers tight around the prize. 'Which hand?'

'The one I can see the dark brown wrapper in, please,' laughed Jamie, reaching up to tap her left hand.

Megan revealed the Mars bar she considered they'd earned and broke it in two, handing the larger piece to Jamie. They sat chewing, trying to make each delicious mouthful last.

'Fancy another game?' asked Jamie.

'Not Monopoly, please, and not the jigsaw,' begged Megan. 'Anything else. Scrabble?'

'I know, how about charades? You should be good at that.'

'Oh I am, I am,' laughed Megan. After all, most of her adult life had been a charade, or so it seemed to her. 'You go first.'

Even from his sitting position, Jamie's miming was far better than Megan's.

'You know,' she said, 'you ought to get a job as an actor. Ever thought about it?'

'And give up a promising future?' Jamie yawned.

'What exactly is your future?' Megan wanted to know.

'I'd like to give it to medical research,' he said, his grin wide.

Not knowing whether or not he was joking, Megan replied, 'As long as it's not your body, they may well accept you.'

Jamie swiped at her and caught her arm, his hand lingering over the fleecy material of her bathrobe. 'I could do with some extra money, of course. Do you think I'd stand a chance in an audition?'

'When we get out of here, I'll see what I can do. They have quite a few extra parts in the soaps and there are crowd scenes for the films. Quite a few British films are made in Scotland.'

'Have you got an agent?'

'I did before I came here.' Megan made a face. 'After I pulled out of the panto, I didn't let her know where I'd be. I reckon she's sick and tired of me now. There's always someone waiting in the wings.'

'Oh no there isn't,' crowed Jamie.

'Oh yes there is,' responded Megan before joining in with Jamie's laughter. Wiping her eyes and clutching her stomach, she asked, 'Are you always cheerful like this?'

'Usually I am,' he said softly. 'People soon get fed up with a misery guts.'

'Jamie, can I ask you something?'

'Anything you like, you should know that by now.'

'If we weren't stuck here in the middle of nowhere, you'd be with your friends and family. So, given that you're soon going to be back with them, what do you see yourself doing a year from now?'

Blowing out his cheeks, Jamie looked thoughtful. 'I'm happy doing what I'm doing. Of course I'd like to finish my research, having made some real progress, but that's not going to be achieved by this time next year. Do you mean New Year's resolutions, that sort of thing?'

'Yeah, okay, what would *they* be?'

'I'll only tell you if you tell me yours,' he grinned.

'Just get on with it,' Megan chivvied.

'To get fitter I think could be one thing. I might join a gym and spend every evening pumping iron or whatever you do at those places. The problem is I'm always late for things and end up taking the car even short distances when I could just as easily have walked. Your go.'

'I'd like to get fitter as well. I'm thinking of taking up boxing, it's the latest craze. Sandra said she'd come with me if there's a class around our way.'

Jamie chuckled and ducked his head. 'I don't think you need any more tackling skills, Meg. You're a force to be reckoned with already.'

'Perhaps one of the main things I'd like to achieve is another good part. The soap was really cool and I loved it.' Megan's excitement intensified as she spoke. 'A stage play would be great. I'd have to be disciplined, but it's fantastic to be in front of an audience and take them along in the story with you. All that adrenaline. Then reading the reviews next day in the papers, hoping you've done well in the eyes of the media.'

'Did you go to drama school?'

'When I left sixth form, I did a fast-track management course and was all set to be a hotel manager.'

'A high-flyer, eh? Yes, I can see you telling people what to do.' Jamie ducked as a pillow came hurtling towards him.

'Not wanting to blow my own trumpet, I *was* a high-flyer. That's what made Douglas mad with me. He just couldn't understand why I'd thrown it all away and taken up acting.'

'But he knew you were an actress when you met. You said it was at the party for the yoghurt advert.'

'Of course he knew, but that doesn't mean he liked it. When he heard what I'd done before I met him he wanted me to go back to that. He thought it would be more stable and secure. A more suitable career for the partner of Douglas Craigie.'

'But as soon as you heard the roar and smelt the crowd, you could do nothing else.'

'That's it exactly, Mr Know-it-all. That's enough from me, let's have another one from you.'

'Eat healthily. I know you've done your best to show me good nutrition in your kitchen here, but I think I could do with a bit more variety as well as fresh fruit and veg.'

'Please don't. Since being stranded here all I can think of is food. But when we get out I'm going on a healthy-eating regime as well. At one time I thought about renting an allotment, but that's all I did — thought. It would have been fun if Douglas had wanted to do it with me, but he showed no interest at all. In fact he more or less forbade me to have anything to do with it. He said it gave the impression of a hillbilly. Can you believe that?' Megan waited for Jamie's response, but none came. 'Is there anything else *you* want?'

Jamie put his finger to his lips. 'Just one thing, but it's a secret.'

'Oh, Jamie, come on, you've got to tell now. I'll lie awake at night guessing wildly otherwise.'

'No, sometimes you simply have to have secrets.'

They sat in silence, each with their own thoughts.

Eventually, Jamie spoke. 'I want to play another game.'

'Okay, we'll tell each other our favourite romantic leads in films. I'll start.'

'Oh, I wanted to go first.'

Megan ignored him. 'I went to the cinema and my favourite romantic lead was Colin Firth in Bridget Jones's Diary. Did you see that?'

'Me go to a girly film? You betcha.' He winked at her. 'I went to the cinema and your favourite romantic lead was Colin Firth and mine was Cate Blanchett in Elizabeth the First.'

Megan frowned in concentration. 'I

went to the cinema and my favourite romantic lead was Colin Firth and yours was Cate Blanchett. My next one is Orlando Bloom in Pirates of the Caribbean. Over to you.'

'My favourite romantic lead was Colin Firth. Oh no it wasn't; that was yours.' Jamie shook his head. 'I can't concentrate on this. Let's change the game. If you could choose anything, what would you fancy to eat?' He looked across at her.

A dreamy look came into Megan's eyes. 'Fish and chips from the chippie, or a fluffy mushroom omelette with a crispy salad. Followed by steamed treacle sponge or chocolate torte. How about you?'

'Roast beef, Yorkshires, crispy spuds. Spotted dick with custard, rhubarb crumble with thick double cream . . . This is torture. What have we got left? No, don't tell me, I'll go and have a look.' Resolutely he struggled to his feet and grasped the umbrella.

Megan let him go. It was hard to see

him battling with his injury. Briefly she wondered if Douglas had paused in his Christmas celebrations to think of her at all. Jamie thought of his Tami several times a day. Now why did that get under her skin? Was she jealous? Megan couldn't answer her own question. It was one thing to be drawn to someone under circumstances such as this, but what would happen once they were back to their normal routines? For all his cuddles and hand-holding, Jamie wasn't to be taken too seriously, she decided. And she'd admitted to Jamie that if Douglas were to ask her to come back, she still wasn't sure whether or not she would. Was it possible she might at least be tempted? He was still in her mind, so perhaps the answer was yes.

'Christmas cake or Christmas cake,' said Jamie, hobbling back, feeding his face with a piece of icing and marzipan. 'We should give it to the birds.'

'I think it's too cold even for the birds to go far for food,' observed

Megan. 'Are you sure there's nothing else? I did put some tins on the worktop, right at the back.'

'You mean the oxtail soup and chicken in sweet and sour sauce?' He grimaced as he said it.

'I'll mix them together and heat them through. There are still some cookies left; we could have them for breakfast.'

'Cookies and hot water, yummy. I hope I don't oversleep for that treat.' He pulled a face at Megan and her heart unexpectedly thumped as if to tell her something. Well, she wasn't going to listen.

She took her time in the kitchen, gently heating the glutinous concoction. She tried to imagine Jamie in other situations apart from this. She could see him at home with her parents and being very much part of the family. Douglas had always held himself aloof and hadn't wanted to attend her family's celebrations. Often she'd visited them without him because he'd made some excuse about having important work to do or given some other reason not to be there. Her mum hadn't said anything, but her feelings had been clear. And her dad had never known what to say to Douglas — they didn't have anything in common, and their sense of humour differed enormously. Dad could usually find something funny to make the family laugh, but Douglas was rather dour.

'What are you doing, Meg? I'm dying of starvation by a dying fire. No, don't rush in and help. I'll struggle to get some more logs on.'

She didn't reply and waited for the cry of pain. She giggled. Jamie was so much fun even in these dreadful circumstances. But she'd loved Douglas and it was difficult to get over such a strong emotion and forget all the things they'd shared. Even if he had made a dreadful mistake and wanted her back, would she ever be able to trust him again? What would she do? Would she give him a second chance? She told herself not to even think about it. There was no reason why he'd ever contact her. She had to get used to the thought that they were finished with each other forever.

'Meg, is the recipe very complicated?' Jamie called.

She spooned the mixture into bowls and carried it through. 'You'll have to imagine some delicious crusty bread to go with it.'

Jamie took a spoonful. 'Yuck! That has to be the worst thing I've ever tasted.'

'Just eat it and be thankful we've got anything at all to eat.' She too took a mouthful. 'Yuck, yuck, yuck! You're right for once. I can't eat it either.'

They put their bowls down. 'So we'd better have the cookies and hot water now,' Meg suggested, tears welling.

'Don't be upset, Meg. We'll be all right. This weather can't last forever. Let's see if we can get a forecast on the radio.'

Megan fetched the radio and switched it on. There was a slight crackle, then nothing. 'What's wrong with the wretched thing?' she said, shaking it.

'It's probably the batteries. Not to worry, we'll know when it starts to thaw. We'll manage, you'll see. Tell you what, let's have another go at the jigsaw. At least the picture on the front shows sunshine. Let's imagine we're there.' Jamie fished it out from under the bed-settee, adjusting his wonky spectacles in the process. He pointed to the picture of the jigsaw. 'You could be that old lady in the deckchair,' he teased.

'I'm going to be just as rude as you,' responded Megan. She studied the picture. 'I see you as the little boy with the ice cream paddling in the freezing cold sea,' added Megan, cheering up. 'Okay, let's make a start.

After a while, Jamie said, 'I'm getting cramp doing this. Can we have a break?'

'We've done well. You pack it away and I'll get us a drink.'

Megan fetched mugs of hot water and the cookies and sat on the arm of the chair which Jamie was hogging. She tried to take her mind off the pangs of hunger which were unsettling her. 'What is it you do? I know you said something about research. Aren't you a bit old to be a student?'

Jamie adjusted his spectacles to straighten them, but they immediately slid to one side. He didn't want to go into detail about his research work as he knew that once he started going on about it he'd never stop. There was no way he could inflict that on Meg; it wasn't fair to her. She'd had such a rotten Christmas on her own that all he wanted now was for her to have a bit of fun. So he decided on, 'After my gap years I took a science degree, carried on with a masters and then took the opportunity to spend some time doing research. It's exciting; there are so many new breakthroughs. Any advance made is worth all the painstaking work.' Anxious to change the subject, he asked, 'What about you? What have you done?'

'As I said I did a management

course, but acting is all I ever wanted to do. I got a lucky break with the part in *Watch Your Back* and have been busy ever since. We were warned that we'd spend a lot of time waitressing, but I've been fortunate.'

'Or maybe it's because you're talented.'

'I'm not sure about that. There are plenty of people auditioning and if you're not reliable there's always someone to take your place. Maybe some burger bar will take me on when I get home.'

'I'd take you on.'

Megan wasn't sure what he meant and she couldn't see his eyes because he was gazing into the fire. 'Jamie, I feel as though I've known you far longer than a few days. You're like an old friend I can say anything to.'

'Go on, you're itching to ask me something personal.'

'I'm just curious. Do you think you'll ever get over Tami and love someone else?'

'Definitely.'

Megan realised that was all he was going to say on the subject so she dropped it. But Jamie had his serious face on as he looked at her and said, 'And you'll get over Douglas too. You may not think so now, but in time you'll see things differently. I hope you'll be happy.'

'Thanks.' Megan felt awkward and didn't know what to say, but wanted to lighten the mood. 'Do you know who you look like?'

'Rupert Everett, Brad Pitt, Leonardo di Caprio?'

'A geek.'

Jamie removed his spectacles and checked the repair. 'It's a sophisticated look.'

It was the last word she'd use to describe Jamie, but he was definitely captivating. Douglas was sophisticated. Thinking of him made her want to check her phone just in case by some fluke the weather conditions had changed and there was now a signal.

But she didn't want Jamie to know what she was doing.

'I think I'll clean my teeth. We might as well get to sleep now.' She took her phone into the bathroom, but there was still no signal. When she went back Jamie had pulled the bed out and was tucking in the bedding.

'It's odd sharing a bed with a stranger,' she said.

'They used to do it all the time in the old days. When you arrived at an inn you never knew who you'd be sharing with. It could be somebody really smelly.' He smiled at her.

'You're not suggesting . . . '

'No, but I might have to sleep at the other end of the room in a couple of days.' He sat on the edge of the bed. 'But I'm not a stranger now, am I, Meg?'

'In some ways yes, and in some ways no.'

'If I'd met you at a club or salsa evening and had asked you out, what would you have said?'

Megan didn't know what to say. Why was he asking her that? She made a joke of his question. 'No thanks, not until you'd been to dance classes. Budge out of the way. I bagsy the sleeping bag again as you pinch all the covers.' She burrowed into the sleeping bag and listened to the comforting sound of Jamie whistling in the bathroom. If he hadn't turned up she didn't know how she would have survived. But did she just see him as simply her saviour, or did her feelings run deeper?

Jamie bounced his way into a comfortable position.

'It's like sharing with a frog.' Megan giggled.

'I know you said this back-to-back business was the best way to keep warm, but it's not very friendly.' More bouncing later and Jamie had turned over and put his arm round her. 'That's better. You don't mind, do you?'

'No, I don't mind.' And she didn't mind at all. She felt happy and at ease lying in the arms of the nicest man she'd ever met. She turned her head and kissed his cheek. He sighed contentedly and they were both soon blissfully asleep.

9

Megan dreamt she was on a lorry roaring down a motorway towards the sun. The noise of the traffic woke her and she surfaced from the snug envelope of Jamie's sleeping bag. She held her breath and listened. Something was out there, but she couldn't imagine what. As she tried not to disturb Jamie, she slipped from the bed and hurried to the door, yanking it open. The sound increased and she looked up to see a helicopter hovering above the cottage. Someone must have sent an SOS to the emergency services. There was no time to put on either boots or a coat. Waving with both arms and projecting her voice in a way any actor would be jealous of, she ran about in the snow, desperately hoping she would be seen or heard. The helicopter dived a little. As hope rose, it was snatched away. She hadn't been seen. Feeling defeated by the lost chance, Megan went back into the cottage.

'What's up, Meg?' Jamie was disentangling himself from the bed clothes and reaching for the umbrella crutch.

'There was a helicopter. I did my best, but it didn't see me,' she sniffed.

'What was it doing around here, do you suppose?' He came over to her and patted her shoulder with his free hand.

'Looking for us — obviously.' Taking a deep breath, Megan said, 'It could have been Douglas. He might have tried to phone me and when I didn't answer, he was worried and called out the emergency services.' Megan knew a poor motivation when she heard one, especially from her own lips. She snatched her gran's red jumper from the back of the chair. It was still a bit damp, but it was a good colour in which to be spotted. When the helicopter came over again, she'd be prepared. Then she tried to sort through the various pieces of clothing scattered around the bed and floor.

'Your feet are soaking, Meg. Here, put these on.' He flung the pair of socks with the vulgar message on towards her.

'I'm not wearing those,' she said, throwing them back towards him. But no others were readily available. 'Okay, let's have them, at least they're dry.' She sat on the chair to change her socks and pull on her boots.

Jamie had also got dressed for the outdoors and when they heard the helicopter whining once more, they were out of the door like greyhounds from a trap.

'Help, here we are,' shrieked Megan, taking up her hopping and skipping once again, hoping the red would be seen.

At length, Jamie said, 'It's no good, Meg, it's gone again. I don't think they're looking for us.' He started back towards the cottage door. Then, 'Hey, what's that for?' Megan had lobbed a large, icy snowball at him and caught him square on his jaw.

She grinned at him and threw another one, catching his face. When his spectacles fell into the snow it didn't deter her. She rained snowball after snowball towards him.

'Right, Miss Meg, you've asked for it.' After retrieving his spectacles, he gathered a large ball, packed it down hard and threw it towards her. She ducked and the snowball fell at her feet. Rolling it along, it increased in size. 'You're not going to get me with that, are you?' asked Jamie, pointing to the mega-sized ball of snow.

'No, I'm going to do *this*.' She continued with her rolling and patting of the snow until it was huge. 'Come on, you can help. We're building a snowman.'

'I haven't had my breakfast yet,' moaned Jamie.

'If you remember, you had it last night. There's precious little left, except water.' She resolved not to mention the Mars bar or the half-packet of cookies hidden in the cupboard until later. They were to be brought out only if the situation got really grim and they were sizing each other up for a final meal.

Jamie shrugged and scooped a bit more snow onto the snowman before edging back to admire it. 'It looks magnificent,' he enthused, 'but a bit bare.' He hobbled back to the cottage, returning in a trice with something held behind his back. 'Don't look,' he called.

Megan turned away and waited patiently.

'Okay, you can peep now.'

'Oh, Jamie, you wretch. You've ruined them.' Megan giggled as she looked at the snowman, or rather snow woman, considering that he'd dressed her in the snazzy underwear Jamie had worn at their celebration Christmas meal.

'We worked out they're not your size, and they didn't really suit me,' said Jamie, picking up a handful of snow and rubbing it into Megan's face.

She spluttered away the icy crystals. 'Do you know, I'm so cold, I can't even feel that.'

'Your face is pink.' Jamie inspected it. 'Hope you don't get frostbite.' Then, abruptly, he was down in the snow on his back.

'What now?' asked Megan, her hands on her hips. 'Really, you are a complete and utter calamity.' She watched as Jamie scissored his arms and legs — well, one leg only.

'I'm an angel,' he cried.

'Don't flatter yourself,' tutted Megan. 'Get up, you'll catch your death.'

Jamie flopped over onto his side. 'Haven't you ever done this?'

'Do I look like a mad woman to you? Oh, okay, don't answer that.' She stooped down so her face was next to his. 'Explain yourself.'

'You've spoilt it now.' He pointed to her footprints. 'The pattern I'm making is supposed to be that of an angel with wings.'

'Ah, how sweet,' replied Megan, lying down on her back. 'I want a go.' She repeated the movements she'd seen Jamie performing. 'Is this right?'

Jamie struggled to get upright and held out the end of the umbrella. 'Grab the end of this and I'll help you get up. Take care, you don't want to spoil the pattern.'

Gingerly Megan let Jamie haul her to a standing position. Together they gazed at the snow before them. 'It's beautiful,' breathed Megan.

Jamie cupped Megan's chin in his gloved hand. 'You're an angel, Meg.'

Standing in the snow getting their breath back, Megan asked, 'Do you think that helicopter will come back? It *could* have been looking for us.' She tried to convince herself that was the case, although she knew in her heart that Douglas wouldn't call the police or mountain rescue or whoever it was responsible for seeking out lost people.

'Let's go in, Meg.' Jamie put an arm around her shoulders and guided her back to the cottage.

'You're covered in snow and soaking wet.' Megan brushed at Jamie's clothes. 'Have you anything dry to change into?'

'We'll manage. There must be something. Not expecting posh visitors, are we?'

'Everything's just a joke to you.' Megan tried to smile, but it was getting increasingly difficult with all the problems they had to face.

Back inside, Jamie heated a large pan of snow. 'I'll empty this into the bathroom sink for you to have a nice hot wash. You'll feel transformed.'

Megan eagerly gathered the scented bath things her mother had given her and enjoyed her time in the improvised beauty parlour of the small, chilly bathroom. It also gave her a while to try and get her head around a few things.

She liked Jamie's company and in this situation he was the best; he kept her spirits up. If only she could stop thinking about Douglas, but it wasn't possible just yet. She'd been convinced they were made for each other and they'd shared so much. She still remembered the good times before he'd treated her so despicably. Things were quite different now from what she'd planned for Christmas. She was snowbound with a stranger. That made her snort with laughter, as she no longer imagined Jamie as a stranger of any sort; he was a boy-next-door type, although sometimes when she looked at him she was surprised by the effect he had on her.

The hot water soothed her and it was bliss to immerse her hair in it and feel the grime and grease floating away. She wrapped her snug bathrobe around her and looked in vain for a spare towel to wrap around her wet hair. There was no alternative but to dry it in front of the fire.

'If you sit here I'll dry your hair for you,' Jamie said, waving a towel around.

So that was where the spare towel had got to. She did as he'd asked and let him gently rub her hair. She closed her eyes as he massaged her scalp. Letting herself relax, she continued to think about Douglas. Where had she gone wrong; why had he been attracted to someone else when she'd been so sure they had a special bond? Then she tried to think of when he'd ever done anything like this for her. He'd given her vouchers for treatments at the spa and treated her to expensive haircuts, but had he ever dried her hair or massaged her feet? She giggled.

'What's tickled you?' Jamie asked as he brushed her hair and tried to style it by curling it round his fingers.

'Nothing.'

'Go on, tell, or I'll be rough with your tangles.'

'I was just hoping you'd massage my feet.'

'Is this some kind of test? You know, if I don't pass you'll never let me be stranded in a cottage with you ever again? Of course I'll massage your feet. Are they clean?'

Megan grabbed the towel and threw it at him. 'Cheek!'

'If you lie on the settee and take your delightful socks off I'll see what I can do. I'm a pretty good masseur, but lack of food might have a negative effect.'

He looked so forlorn with his bandaged spectacles, but it was impossible not to laugh at him. Douglas would never ridicule himself like Jamie did. She found it endearing. 'Let's use the potions my mum gave me. There must have been some massage oil or foot cream.'

Jamie limped off to the bathroom and called out, 'We could probably eat half this lot. How do you fancy Hot Chilli and Mustard foot oil?'

'Mmm, yummy.'

Jamie returned shaking the bottle. 'It boosts circulation so you won't have cold feet after this. Ready?'

Meg dozed contentedly and it was some time later when she awoke to find herself tucked under the covers. Her feet were like toast; Jamie had somehow put the awful socks back on without waking her. He was sitting in the armchair reading.

'What's that you're engrossed in?'

'*Massage for Experts*. Not that I need to read it.'

'Truthfully.'

'*How to Dig Yourself out of a Snowdrift.*'

'Jamie!'

'It's a book of carols. I found it between *ICT Explained* and *Family History Branch by Branch*. I've been thinking we need to cheer ourselves up, so a session of singing might be just the answer.'

Megan wasn't so sure. She'd already heard his rendition of 'We Wish You a Merry Christmas'. But she wasn't going to dampen his enthusiasm so would plainly have to put up with it.

'Favourite carol?' he asked.

'While shepherds washed their socks . . . '

'I'll count us in: one, two, three.'

Much laughter and singing later, Jamie said, 'I think we need some musical instruments for accompaniment. Are you any good on the spoons, Meg? Or is your expertise in the comb and paper?'

'Definitely spoons. I'll get them.'

'No, you stay tucked up in bed.'

Watching Jamie gather up a selection

of instruments, Megan wondered what Sandra and her other friends would think if they could see her now. It was the most ludicrous situation, but she was having more fun than she could remember in a long time. She knew she would have managed even if Jamie hadn't turned up, but it would have been a very different situation. Sandra would say Jamie's arrival at the cottage was fate.

'Ready for 'The Holly and the Ivy?' ' Jamie said enthusiastically.

But after several more carols even he began to flag. 'I'm really hungry, Meg. Is there nothing to eat at all?'

'There might be a chocolate left in the box. It's on the table.'

Jamie shambled over to have a look. 'No, nothing except a few empty wrappers.'

He looked so despondent she had to tell him about the secret supply of cookies and the Mars bar.

'Shall we eat them now?' he asked excitedly.

'If we do we'll have nothing left. Maybe we should wait a bit.'

'What happened to the dates? The ones Sandra gave you. I haven't eaten them, have you?'

'Brilliant idea. I'd completely forgotten about them too. Maybe they're in one of the bags I brought my presents in.'

They both leapt up and scrambled around until Jamie cried elatedly, 'I've got them!'

'Would sir like some hot water to go with his five-star repast?'

When she brought the mugs of steaming water she joined Jamie on the settee. He sipped, rolled the liquid round his mouth and declared, 'A good vintage. Slightly oaky flavour with a touch of berry and spice.'

As Megan pulled one of the sticky dates out of the box, she half-believed they would both end up completely mad if they didn't get away soon.

'Take your time, relish each one,' Jamie advised as he gulped down the sweet fruit. 'I can't believe how hungry I feel. We take so much for granted and forget how lucky we are.'

'What do you mean? Lucky to be stuck here in the middle of nowhere with hardly any food, no running water and a dwindling supply of firewood?'

'Lucky to be together at least. When I was locked out and spotted your cottage, I never imagined who the occupant would be. It's a bit like Hansel and Gretel.'

'So you think I'm a witch who cooks people and eats them?' She grabbed his arm and made munching noises.

'Okay, maybe not Hansel and Gretel, maybe Snow White. You know when the handsome prince turns up? That's me.' He pointed his finger at himself. 'He kisses Snow White and she wakes up.'

'I wasn't asleep when you arrived.'

'But . . . '

'But what?'

'But nothing.' Jamie put his mug on the floor before taking her hands in both of his. 'It's strange how things change. Since being here in the cottage with you I've hardly thought of Tami. I feel guilty in a way, but also free. I've realised it's time to move on. Until meeting you I thought I'd never meet anyone special. Tami's no longer in here all the time.' He tapped his head.

With her own emotions in turmoil, Megan couldn't face a heavy conversation with him so tried to change the subject. 'That's because you've had food on your mind.'

'No, it isn't. It's because I've had you on my mind.' He put his arm round her.

'There's not much else to think about here, just each other.'

'It isn't just that. Surely you feel something too? Some sort of connection.'

Megan didn't answer. She didn't know what to say.

He turned her face to his and tenderly stroked her cheek. 'Meg, I've been so restrained I'm quite proud of myself.'

Megan could hear the tension in his voice and longed to reassure him. She wanted to take him in her arms and kiss his anxieties away. Jamie took her mug and placed it on the floor next to his. Caressing her, he brought his lips to meet hers in a long lingering kiss. Megan experienced a wave of happiness cascading inside her and responded. She felt the beat of his heart next to hers as their kisses became more urgent. But all too soon Jamie pulled away. Disappointment flooded through her. Jamie had done what she hadn't had the willpower to do.

* * *

Megan was getting used to being awake long before Jamie stirred, but looking at her watch she was shocked to find it was past mid-day. She slipped out of the sleeping bag and padded to the bathroom, taking her phone with her. Last night had been hideous. They'd both been uneasy after their shared kiss and it was a relief to be able to hide in the darkness in bed under the covers.

Megan was convinced that their isolated situation was to blame for Jamie imagining himself drawn to her. If she were honest, she'd own up to liking him and having had a wonderful time since he'd landed on her doorstep. But she was on the rebound and so, regardless of what he'd said, was he. If they'd met at a party in her home town they may have exchanged a few pleasantries and gone their separate ways. Considering everything that was going on, it was madness for either of them to draw any conclusions as to how they felt about each other.

Without consciously thinking about it, Megan turned the tap and was startled but thrilled when water dribbled through it. Hastily she stuck the plastic plug into the hole. Today she wanted a wash with water from the tap, even if it was cold. And it certainly was that. Shivering as she tried to dry herself on the still-damp towel, her phone emitted a squeak. Grabbing it, she pressed the green button and several text messages flagged up.

One was from Douglas. Scanning it, she knew then that it wasn't he who had called the helicopter to rescue her; he'd sent the message on Boxing Day just hoping she'd had a merry Christmas and he'd be in touch with her in the New Year. Well, the New Year started tomorrow. Rapidly her mind switched into gear and she knew she'd have to be proactive in getting out of this cottage and back to civilisation. She must put Jamie and this surreal holiday out of her head.

'Meg, Meg, can you hear that?' Jamie was knocking on the bathroom door. 'The snow's melting. The thaw has started.'

Megan emerged from the bathroom with the tatty towel around her and together they listened to the drip, drip of the outside world. 'At last! That's fantastic. Now we'll be able to get out of here.' Megan jumped up and down. Then there was another sound; someone was at the front door. Hastily, Megan dashed back into the bathroom while Jamie answered the knock. She held her breath as she tried to hear what was being said, but could only make out mutterings of a conversation and then the door was slammed shut.

'You can come out now, Meg. You'll never believe what I've got here.' Megan's eyes widened as she saw the box Jamie was holding. 'It's your welcome hamper,' he said with a grin. 'Let's see what's in it.'

Together they shuffled to the kitchen, Jamie carrying the box and Megan excitedly trying to ransack it. When it was on the kitchen worktop, they laid out the sumptuous contents in a row.

'Are the roads clear, then?' asked Megan, still finishing dressing. She pulled her jumper down and adjusted her belt. 'I've lost weight, so the holiday wasn't a complete waste of time.' She grinned up at Jamie and caught his devastated expression. 'Look, I didn't mean . . . '

'Eggs, there are eggs in here,' exclaimed Jamie, returning his attention to the box, but his voice wasn't quite steady. 'And milk and tea.'

'I'll use this,' said Megan, taking out a large bottle of water and pouring some into the kettle. 'Gosh, what a luxury. I never thought I'd come to think of water in those terms.' Then she rummaged around for a large frying pan and put some butter in it along with some bacon rashers they had also found.

'Um, that smells divine,' observed Jamie. 'What did you mean about the roads, Meg?'

'The person who brought this — ' She nodded towards the box. ' — which way did he come? It would have been good to know if all the roads were clearing or just in one direction.'

Jamie banged his forehead with his hand. 'Dope, aren't I? I didn't even think of that. He just said he couldn't get through with this on Christmas Eve because his four-by-four had a puncture and he hoped that it wasn't too late to deliver it now. I just grabbed it from him, thanked him and shut the door.'

'Never mind. Can't do much about it now.' Megan continued with cooking the breakfast and when they at last sat in front of the fading fire, huge plates of food before them and large mugs of tea with milk and sugar beside them, Megan said, 'We must start to pack up after we've finished this.'

'Anxious to be on your way?' Jamie got out between shovelling forkfuls of breakfast into his mouth.

'Of course I am,' replied Megan. 'Aren't you?'

'Sort of,' he said. 'But I've had a good time here.' He put his empty plate on the floor and lifted his mug. 'To you, Meg. Thanks for everything.'

Megan waited for his quip, but it didn't come. Perhaps he was preparing himself for the real world, too. He might, as a rule, be the most boring, serious person around for all she knew. She didn't want him to disappear from her life altogether, which would be sad after all they'd shared. What was also sad was that she didn't even know his last name. In fact, she knew precious little about him now she came to think of it.

* * *

Jamie busied himself in the kitchen, washing up and tidying things, while Megan folded the bedclothes and reverted the bed into a settee. Without really knowing why, she threw a couple more logs onto the fire and poked at them, as she thought about the days ahead. She didn't hear Jamie come through to the living room until he said, 'Would you mind if I stayed here a bit longer after you've gone?'

'But why?' Megan frowned.

Shrugging, he said, 'I expect you'll think I'm a big baby, but I'm not sure I can drive. My ankle's still a bit sore.'

'I hadn't given it a thought,' cried Megan. 'Oh, Jamie, why didn't you say something?'

'I just have.' He smiled.

'I'll stay with you. Or I could give

you a lift. Yes that's it, I'll give you a lift.'

Jamie shook his head. 'I'd only have to come back for the car, because I'm lost without it. Anyway, someone has to stay and finish the jigsaw — or shall we break it up and put it back in the box for you to take with you?'

'No, that's fine, you carry on. If you're determined to stay here, just lock the door and push the key back through the letterbox. That's what they said to do when I left.'

Jamie nodded and looked around the room. 'So are you going to pack now? What can I do to help?'

Things were going sour and Megan couldn't bear it. 'Do you think we can meet up? I only live a few miles from Edinburgh; I'm often there.'

'I don't know,' replied Jamie. 'Let's wait and see what happens when we get back. Things may look different then and you may not want to meet up with me again.'

Megan had never known him this

gloomy. Even when he hurt his ankle, his loud moans and groans of self-pity were more bearable than how he was behaving now. 'Let's at least exchange phone numbers,' she pleaded.

'Sure. Do you think the phones are working yet?'

'Yes, I had a text from Douglas,' Megan blurted out, before realising it was the wrong thing to say.

'That's nice.' Jamie smiled. 'I expect he was worried about you. I'm sure he would have rung you to wish you a good time over Christmas. He must be important to you.'

Things weren't going well at all and Megan didn't like it. She threw open her suitcase and folded her things into it. 'I've got texts from loads of my family and friends. Some of them sound quite anxious as they haven't heard from me at all. My mum sounds especially worried. I'm usually good at keeping in touch.'

'You'll be able to reply to her now.'

'I've already done that. As soon as I

found we had a signal I replied.' Megan looked round the room. 'Would you like the decorations left up if you're staying on?'

'I don't mind,' said Jamie, picking up the book he had been reading the day before and sitting in the armchair.

'At least you'll have food,' Megan said. When he didn't reply, she begged, 'Jamie, please don't be like this. We've been thrown together by an odd set of circumstances, we made the best of it and now we've got to go our separate ways. It would be nice to meet up, but if you don't want to see me again, I do understand.'

'Okay,' said Jamie, sounding a bit more like his animated self, 'how about we meet up a year from now? Where could it be? Not here. I'm not sure I'd find it again.'

'You're on. We can arrange where later,' Megan said with a smile. A year was a long time, but at least he'd agreed to meet. Also, she had his phone number so she could easily get in touch with him at any time. However, in the last hour, she'd felt a bit shy and was reluctant to push herself on him.

'I hope your car starts without a lot of trouble,' Jamie said.

'Oh, I hadn't thought of that.'

'Don't take this the wrong way, but would you like me to see if it'll start?'

'You said you couldn't drive with your ankle like that,' Megan objected.

'We could just see if it starts first. If you let me have the keys, you can stay here by the fire.'

'No, you give me your keys and let me see if both cars work. I'm not leaving you here if your car won't start.'

Jamie threw her his keys and turned back to his book.

* * *

When Megan returned, she wasn't alone. 'Look who's here.'

'Pity you didn't come in the first place. Meg was trapped here for several days.'

'I hardly ever spend Christmas with Megan, do I, Sis?'

'Oh, this is your *brother*.' Jamie stood up and shook hands.

'Yes. What on earth have you come all the way here for in these awful conditions, Tommy?' Megan asked.

'Mum insisted. She phoned me and said I had to check up on you, make sure you were all right, because she said you'd never not get in touch on Christmas Day. I told her you'd be fine with Douglas, but she said she had a bad feeling about it.'

'I sent her a message just now, as soon as we got a signal.'

'Wasted journey then. So where *is* Douglas?' Tommy peered round the room.

'He didn't come with me. He had something else to do.'

Tommy raised his eyebrows, but Megan didn't add anything more. 'And you are?' he asked.

'Jamie.'

'And you're a friend of Megan's who

came with her because Douglas was busy?'

'No, I was locked out of my cottage. We've been keeping each other company.'

Tommy looked round the small room. 'I see.' He winked at Megan.

'It's not what you think, Tommy. Don't judge everyone by your own standards. Would you like something to eat and drink?' Megan asked, pleased that they had something decent to offer.

'I stopped at a hotel just down the road. I wasn't sure how much longer it would take me to get here. Actually, I'm on my way to yet another party. I just had to detour a bit. But as you seem to be perfectly fine, I'll be off. Let's meet up when you get back and have a New Year's drink. Happy New Year, and drive carefully,' he said, kissing her on the cheek. 'Happy New Year to you too, Jamie.'

'Yes, great, same to you.'

After Tommy had gone, Megan turned to Jamie. 'That was so lovely of him to bother to check up on me. I know it was Mum's idea, but he didn't have to do what she said.'

'It *was* nice of him. Pity he didn't want to stay longer, but I expect he's sampled your cooking before.'

'Very funny. I'm going to have to dig a way down the lane to get my car out. The road's not too bad — there have been a couple of vehicles down there including Tommy's, so there are track marks to follow, but there's no way I can get down to the road without clearing some of the snow. Your car started fine, but we'll leave it running for a bit. Mine started too, so we're both okay to get out of here.'

Jamie was already up and putting his jacket on. 'There are a couple of spades in the outhouse. I'll fetch those.'

They both put their backs into the work and a while later Megan's car was loaded with her things and parked on the road.

Jamie leaned on his spade, resting his injured ankle. 'You'll come back up to the cottage for some hot soup and buttered toast? You've a long journey ahead of you.'

Megan didn't want to prolong things. She didn't know what might be said or unsaid that they'd regret later. 'No, I think I'd better be off. Bye, Jamie, see you.' She gave him a quick peck on the cheek and jumped into her car.

'Wait a minute, I've got something for you. It's a Christmas present.' He reached into his pocket and pulled out a tiny parcel, wrapped in a tissue daubed with coloured spots and tied with a ribbon.

She took the gift and studied it. 'I love the wrapping. It's amazing what you can do with nothing.' She tugged at the ribbon. Pulling off the tissue, she found an intricately carved and decorated wooden snowman. 'It's got arms, a hat and a broom. How incredible and beautiful. When did you make it? I had no idea.'

'When you were busy doing other things in the kitchen or bathroom, when you were fetching wood, and sometimes when you were asleep at night. I used the tools on my new fancy penknife. And I have to confess I pinched some of your nail polishes to paint on the face and buttons.'

'I don't know what to say. I'll treasure this. It will remind me of all the fun we've had together and how lucky I was that you were the one who turned up out of the blizzard.'

'It could have been the abominable snowman.'

'Let's go back up to the cottage, I want to give you something too.'

Jamie's face lit up and he limped after her up the lane. She stopped by the snow woman.

'I'm going to use your phone to take your photo with the snow woman. Then when you get back you can transfer it to your computer, print it off and frame it. What's the matter?' Megan could see that Jamie was disappointed.

'What I'd really like would be a photo of you with the snow woman.

Look, if you stand here that would be perfect. Put your arm round her.' Jamie prepared to take the picture.

'Wait. Let me hold the little snow-man in my other hand. Can you see him?'

'Yes, perfect. Say haggis.'

'Haggis,' she said, grinning.

10

With a cheery wave Megan was off. She had to concentrate hard on her driving, as the road was treacherous in places, and it was only when she stopped miles later for a break that she had time to think about Jamie. Tucking into a baked potato in a pub, she wondered what he would be doing stuck in the cottage on his own. She imagined him engrossed in his book, his broken spectacles balanced on his nose. As she pictured him, warmth swept through her body. She felt terrible about leaving him, especially on New Year's Eve, but told herself it was for the best.

And what was she going to do when she got back to her flat? She'd be on her own too. She'd refused all party invitations because she'd thought she and Douglas would still be at the cottage enjoying their romantic break.

A little voice told her to go back and celebrate with Jamie. But a louder voice told her to face reality. Jamie couldn't possibly feel anything for her; he'd been reluctant to meet up with her again — and wasn't she still in love with Douglas even though he had no feelings for her? She finished her meal and continued her journey.

* * *

If there had been anyone around to ask, there was no way Megan would have been able to describe the luxury of a bath filled with hot water and overflowing with bubbles. Or the cosiness of a centrally heated flat. She had her portable CD player in the bathroom playing some of her favourite music, a bar of chocolate she'd found in the fridge, and a bestseller to read. Her little snowman was sitting on the window ledge reminding her of Jamie, and she should have been content. She still hadn't told anyone she was back home. She didn't want any sympathy, and why did she need any? The last few days had been spent in primitive conditions, but with a man who'd made even that experience enjoyable. Lying in the bath, Megan relived the feelings she'd had when she and Jamie had kissed. Her mobile phone rang, interrupting her reflections. After checking who it was, she answered.

'Hello, Douglas.' She felt strangely disappointed to hear his voice. She used to feel goosebumps when she spoke to him. 'Yes, I'm back . . . Meet up with you? What, tonight? Why . . . ? But you dumped me for your new woman. What's going on? Do you really think I'm going to come running back to you after the way you treated me? No, I won't calm down. You've no idea how I feel. Yes, I'll think about seeing you, but not tonight. I suppose we could meet up for a drink sometime. I'll get in touch. What — you're offering me a job in your office? I'm an actress, Douglas, not an administrator. Of course I hope to continue with my acting career.' She tossed the phone on the floor. She was seething. How dare he? Spotting her little snowman grinning from the window ledge, she calmed down. Yes, she would meet up with Douglas, if only to have closure. Then perhaps she'd be able to move on.

* * *

It was strange how she was lying in the most comfortable bed and yet couldn't sleep. Perhaps it was the lack of Jamie's reassuring presence. She clicked the light on again to check the time. It was almost two. Her snowman stood illuminated on the bedside table. She would treasure it more than any gift of expensive jewellery or perfume. Disappointed and slightly worried not to hear from Jamie, she had stayed up until after midnight just in case he got in touch. She would have hoped he would wish her a Happy New Year even though she'd left him to fend for himself. It seemed like a case of out of sight out of mind. It hadn't taken him long to forget all about her.

* * *

Although weather conditions weren't anywhere near as appalling as they'd been at the cottage, icy snow still flurried in Scotland. In order to make it up to her agent, Megan paid her a visit, taking with her the perfume Douglas had given her for Christmas. In return, Megan was rewarded with two auditions: the one for the major advertising company she'd been told about before Christmas, and then the most fantastic thing of all — an audition for a play in Edinburgh. Delighted, she skipped back home, pulling Jamie's woolly scarf up round her face and stopping only to purchase a *Big Issue* from the man standing on his usual draughty corner.

Her flat felt chilly when she arrived home, but she'd endured far worse conditions, she told herself, remembering her days with Jamie in the snowbound cottage. All she had to do here was turn the thermostat up. Clutching the scarf to herself, she thought how great it would be to share her news with someone. Although she'd made arrangements to meet up with Douglas that evening, Megan knew he wouldn't be interested in her good fortune. Jamie would, though. And now she had the perfect reason to get in touch with him. She still had his scarf. Fingering the phone, she dithered. He might even have forgotten who she was by now. If he did remember, he might not want to meet her. But she could parcel the scarf up and send it to him if he gave her an address.

* * *

The dinner with Douglas was disastrous. Megan was on tenterhooks as the wine bottle was scrutinised and grudgingly accepted by him. Twice she'd nearly called him Jamie, who seemed to be constantly on her mind; and when the seemingly interminable date finally came to its conclusion, she was glad to get away, assuring Douglas that he needn't escort her in the taxi.

More than ever, she wanted to speak to Jamie. She had absolutely no romantic feelings for Douglas and not even the squeak of a friendship was left now. That particular ghost had been laid to rest. Smiling to herself, she reached for the phone. Then she put it back in her bag. She couldn't go through with it. It was up to Jamie to ring her if he wanted to get in touch. He hadn't even bothered to wish her a Happy New Year. After much pacing and agonising, she judged that a text would be the best option. Nervously she keyed in the message.

* * *

Some days later Megan was strutting the streets of Edinburgh, euphoric that the auditions had gone well and she'd been hired for the play as well as the advert. She was determined not to be upset that Jamie hadn't answered her text message and with a resolute lifting of her chin, she set about being a tourist in the town until it was time to meet her friend. It was a new year and she was ready to make a new start. But knowing that Jamie lived here made her imagine she saw him everywhere. The fourth time she was sure she spotted him from behind. She grinned to herself, as the man in question was smartly dressed and wearing a long black overcoat, and she could imagine Jamie with his hair in that sexy buzz cut. The man turned to check the road before he crossed. Megan stood stock-still, causing a minor pedestrian jam around her. Of course it wasn't him — she would just have to put Jamie out of her mind and get on with a life without him. There could be a good future to look forward to if she put her heart into it.

But before she could put him out of her mind completely, she had a date with her friend Sandra, who wanted to know everything about her Christmas adventure.

'You mean you stayed in the cottage with a complete stranger?' Sandra exclaimed.

'He's a lovely person and absolutely gorgeous-looking.' Megan tried not to conjure a picture of him.

'Whatever! You must be mad. Promise me you'll never even think of doing anything as foolish again.'

Sandra had her mother-hen face on and Megan knew she disapproved. 'He's perfectly harmless.'

'You're lucky to have got home safely. Now I insist we sort out boxing classes. He could have been a mad axe man on the loose. We'll start looking straight away. Here, you look through the local paper and I'll search on the internet.'

Megan laughed and hoped that the two of them would go together. Megan was eager to attend the classes, hoping to get rid of a lot of anger with her sparring partner. Yes, she *was* angry: angry at Douglas for letting her down, and at Jamie for not getting in touch with her. But Megan never got to the classes, as the rehearsals for the play became her focus.

For some reason Megan was having terrible difficulty with pre-play nerves one evening. Normally she would get on the stage and enjoy performing. Rehearsals had been good and she had been overwhelmed with the praise heaped upon her by the director and other actors. It was a well-written comedy and she still found herself laughing at the lines even though she'd heard them a thousand times.

'You look terrible, Megan,' her opposite number said.

'Thanks,' she replied, sweat breaking out on her brow. She took deep breaths, had a sip of water and felt a bit better.

As she wasn't due on stage until half an hour into the first act, she did her favourite thing of peeping through the side curtains and watching the audience's reaction. The auditorium was full of laughing, smiling faces. Not a sweet paper could be heard rustling nor a person seen trying to escape outside before the end. She felt calmer and in control. Her cue came and she was ready.

The first half went very smoothly and the cast was ready for another triumphant night's performance. They'd definitely earned the title of 'best play I've seen in a long time' in a piece by the local critic.

Just into the second half, the audience ready in their seats, none leaving it until the last minute to take their place, Megan began her favourite speech. In it she had to address the audience and pretend they were the members of a jury. Usually she chose one person who she played to — someone sitting stage left approximately a dozen rows back. She knew Douglas was in the audience that night, but she wasn't bothered about his reaction as he'd never thought much of her stage career. But she certainly wasn't prepared for another familiar face which appeared before her. She was sure it was Jamie. She blinked and forgot a word, made one up, looked again. It had to be him, although he looked different. What was he doing here? She forgot another word and her mind was blank. A cue came from the wings and she picked it up, moving her eyes to a different place. But the mood had gone and she struggled. Sympathetically the cast tried to help her out and, at last, she limped into the final scene.

11

The applause was enthusiastic, but Megan knew she hadn't given her best and was mad at herself. It was no good trying to apologise, as the others would say that it was just one of those things and other phrases to make her feel good. Quickly she removed her make-up and changed into jeans and a sweatshirt before trying to make a quick escape home.

'Megan, I wanted to tell you how much I enjoyed your performance.' Douglas stopped her on the stairs which led to the fire exit.

Megan's eyebrows went up. 'You did, Douglas? Nobody else did and you don't usually give me praise for my acting.'

She didn't like the smirk around his mouth as he said, 'It was what they call 'experimental', wasn't it?'

'Sort of,' squirmed Megan, cross with

herself for wanting to save face, especially with Douglas. A thought suddenly came into her head. Jamie might still be in the theatre. He might be hanging around to see her. 'I must dash. Thanks for coming.' With that she rushed out of the stage door and round through the main entrance into the foyer. It was crowded. People were milling around, collecting their coats from the cloakroom, chatting to friends. As Megan pushed through them a few people nudged each other and pointed at her. There was no way she'd find him in this crowd. She managed to reach the stairs leading to the circle, climbed a couple of steps, then turned and called down, 'Jamie, where are you? Jamie.' It must have been her loudest stage voice as there was a hush and everyone turned to look at her. 'Oh, it doesn't matter,' she said, tears welling in her eyes. Back in the street she searched the throng for his friendly face.

'So, this is where you got to.' Douglas

took her arm. 'Dinner is what you need. I know a nice quiet place near here where we can talk.'

Her emotions in turmoil, Megan allowed herself to be led by Douglas down a side street and into the warmth of a small but expensive-looking restaurant. The head waiter darted over immediately. 'Table for two as usual, Mr Craigie?' Douglas glared at the waiter's faux pas.

'So this is where you bring your new woman, is it, Douglas? Or are there more?'

'Let's be civilised, shall we? Couldn't we just enjoy an evening together for old times' sake?'

Megan knew she was being petulant. Seeing Jamie had disturbed her. She tried to pull herself together and watched Douglas study the label on the bottle of red wine he'd ordered. He went through the usual routine of taking his time tasting the wine, then nodding that it was to his taste. As soon as her glass was filled she took a gulp.

'It's good,' she said.

The meal which Douglas, in his usual controlling way, ordered on Megan's behalf was no doubt well-cooked and definitely expensive, but it turned to sawdust in her mouth as she thought of the quirky meals she'd shared with Jamie at the cottage. And she remembered the laughter they'd shared and Jamie's ever-present optimism and kindness. How was she going to endure the evening with one man whilst longing to be with another?

* * *

Jamie wished now he hadn't been so stupid. He should go home and start again tomorrow. What was he doing sitting in this ridiculously expensive restaurant with its booths and prices that would require a mortgage to pay for a full meal? The waiter had raised his eyebrows when he'd ordered tap water and soup. He'd taken refuge through the nearest welcoming doorway after leaving the theatre. The only thought in his head had been Meg. When he'd seen the advert in the local paper for the play and had seen that she was starring in it he hadn't been able to resist coming to see her. She'd seen him as well. Their eyes had locked, just briefly, and all the feelings he had for her had come surging back to overwhelm him. He must stop torturing himself about her and concentrate on his work.

'Your soup, sir.' The waiter took his starched napkin, shook it out and placed it in his lap.

Another waiter held a basket of rolls. 'Granary, wholemeal or white, sir?'

The roll he chose was carefully placed on his plate with silver tongs. Tucking into the soup, he thought of the oxtail soup and chicken in sweet and sour sauce they'd had at the cottage. How disgusting that had been, but he'd rather eat anything with Meg than be sitting here alone. As soon as he'd eaten the soup he paid and made his way to the door. And there she was, sitting with a man. They were raising their glasses in a toast and Meg was smiling at the man and gazing into his eyes.

'To Douglas and Megan.'

So that was Douglas and they were together again. Hurriedly Jamie left the restaurant, knowing that he would have to put her out of his mind completely.

* * *

Megan knew she'd had too much to drink as soon as she started seeing Douglas in a favourable light. She even began giggling at some of his remarks. Had he really suggested they get back together? At the time she didn't much care. Thoughts of Jamie were receding and she tried to convince herself that she'd been mistaken and it wasn't him she'd seen through the glare of the spotlight.

'Thanks for this, Douglas,' she murmured, reaching out for his hand.

'It was very thoughtful of you.' She slued round in her seat. 'This is a nice place.'

'I knew you'd like it,' said Douglas, lifting her hand and kissing the inside of her wrist. 'More wine?'

'Please.' She held out her glass and slurped at it before placing it unsteadily on the white tablecloth.

* * *

The next morning had Megan swearing to stay away from both alcohol and men. The combination wasn't a good one and she had a thumping head and a queasy stomach. *And* she had a performance to do, although that was not until the evening. She turned over in bed, pulled the duvet over her head and slept.

By early afternoon she was feeling better and hauled herself to the bathroom. The phone ringing annoyed her as she'd just stepped under the shower. She let it ring and then spent some time torturing herself, wondering if it had been Jamie. What a silly thought. Nevertheless, she pulled a towel around her and went to see if a message had been left on voicemail. It had been Douglas. He said he'd ring back.

Tea and toast revived Megan even further and she gave herself a talking-to. She'd already been down the Douglas route in her life and it hadn't ended satisfactorily at all for them. Although she had to admit that if he had gone with her to the cottage for Christmas as arranged, she'd never have met Jamie.

There was a knock at her flat door. She wasn't ready to face Douglas so soon, but reluctantly opened the door a crack. It was Kathryn, her neighbour. 'Hi,' she said. 'Goodness, you look rough.'

'Thanks a bundle. That's all people seem to be able to say to me these days.'

'I've brought that jigsaw back. Sorry it took so long. Have you got any others?'

Megan always had a small pile of them under the bed and they went off to choose one.

'How was the show last night?'

'Okay, I think,' said Megan with a frown. But she wasn't a person to lie to her friends. 'Actually it was horrendous. I fluffed my lines and got sidetracked by a face I thought I saw in the audience.'

'Was it Douglas?'

'No. But I did go out to dinner with him afterwards. What about this one?' Megan pointed to a picture of liquorice allsorts.

'Mmm, not sure. Have you finished the one I gave you for Christmas? You know, the seaside scene. It looked quite hard and I feel like a challenge.'

'I left it with Jamie to finish. He was the guy who turned up at the cottage. I'll get it back though.' Megan considered contacting Jamie on the pretext of asking for the jigsaw. She wondered if he would have left it at the cottage or if he would have dismantled it and taken it home.

'Are you and Douglas back together again, then?' Kathryn asked casually as she picked out two of the jigsaws.

'No! I know him too well to fall into his trap again. He was seeing someone else at the same time as I was going out with him. I told you all that when I came back from the cottage.'

'You might have forgiven him. He's got a lot going for him. He's rich and influential.'

'I'll put the kettle on and make some coffee.' Megan led her friend through to the kitchen and busied herself making the drinks and finding biscuits. 'I couldn't ever trust Douglas again, and anyway . . . '

'Anyway what?' Kathryn probed, as she studied the pictures on the two boxes she'd brought through to the kitchen.

'If you must know, I really like Jamie. We were two strangers thrown together, but we were so right for each other. He was such fun to be with. So different from Douglas, who would have been writing letters of complaint to everyone and making me feel miserable and a failure for choosing such a place.'

'Even Douglas couldn't blame you for the snow. Who could he have written to about that?' The two women chuckled and Kathryn continued, 'So what about this Jamie? Is there something you haven't told me?'

'The person I saw in the audience was Jamie. He put me off and I ruined the performance. I searched for him afterwards and couldn't find him. I wonder why he came to see the play if he doesn't care for me at least a little.'

'Maybe he simply enjoys the theatre. Maybe he was with someone. It does explain things though.' Kathryn felt in her pocket and brought out a crumpled bit of newspaper. 'I wasn't sure about showing you this, but it's better for you to be forewarned rather than someone saying something and taking you by surprise.'

Megan took the paper and read it. It was a broadsheet review of the previous night's performance and she was hammered by the critic. 'This actress has no future in theatre'; 'Over-rated and under-rehearsed'; 'Stay in London if you want good theatre'.

'That's awful — I've let everyone down. I hadn't realised I was such a disaster. It's all Jamie's fault. Why did he have to turn up last night?'

'There's only one person who can answer that. So go on, contact him. Thanks for the coffee.' Kathryn tucked the two boxes under her arm and headed for the front door.

Megan decided to run through the script, as she was determined not to mess things up again. When she was sure she would be word-perfect, it was almost time for her to leave for the theatre. She should concentrate on her career, if she still had one, and put Jamie out of her mind.

12

Jamie sat at his workstation trying to concentrate. Things were getting very complicated and the rest of the staff were edgy.

'We're taking one step forward and two backwards if you ask me,' declared someone.

Jamie stood up. 'It's a trying time for us all. We must do our best. We're very, very near to something quite thrilling.' Despite his heavy heart, he felt a bubble of excitement. He knew they were on the threshold of a major breakthrough in the research they'd spent over two years trying to perfect. He was full of nervous energy and he guessed the others were too. If ever anybody needed to pace, it was him and now. 'I suggest you all take a break. Go shopping, go to the gym, surf the internet, whatever will take your mind away from here.'

Hanging around was something Jamie hated doing. Now they had to wait for the analysis of a selection of cells before they could move forward in their research for a cure of one of the most unforgiving forms of cancer. He ran a hand over his face and thought back to his evening at the theatre. Why on earth hadn't he spoken to Megan? He sighed. It would have made no difference; she was back with Douglas.

After he'd read her roasting by the critics, his heart went out to her. He was sure that he was in some way to blame. She'd been fine — well, better than fine. She'd been funny and gorgeous and flirty, and then it seemed that one look at him had taken all her confidence away. He set off on a brisk walk to fill in his time, resolving to keep well away from the theatre.

He decided he must maintain a calm attitude, especially when the results of the tests came back to his laboratory. His work was at a critical stage; a leap forward was imminent, he was sure.

Turning back the way he'd come, he headed to the laboratory.

* * *

Before going to the theatre, Megan needed a walk and some fresh Scottish air. Over and over in her head went her lines, and she felt in character as she bobbed along the street, lips moving and laughing at the lines as she went.

Her mobile phone vibrated in her pocket and her heart lifted. Maybe Jamie was trying to get in touch with her. Looking at the screen, she tried not to be too disappointed.

'Hi there, sis.' From the background noise it sounded as though Tommy was in a bar.

'Tommy, what's going on?'

'I'm celebrating with some mates.'

Megan was annoyed with herself for forgetting her brother's birthday. She'd been so self-absorbed she hadn't given a thought to anyone else. She'd never missed his birthday before.

'I thought you could meet me after the show and bring my present.'

Megan knew he was teasing, but still felt awful. 'That would be good.'

'Yeah, I thought you might need cheering up.'

She certainly needed that, but Tommy could only be referring to the review. 'Why's that then?'

'I saw the write-up in the paper from that critic. I remember you telling me he knows what he's talking about, so you must be pretty upset. Hold on. Cheers, mate!'

Megan could imagine him surrounded by his friends and looked forward to being part of their warm group. 'Tell me where you are and I'll get there as soon as I can after the performance.'

She tried to think of a gift she could get before seeing him, but couldn't concentrate. Tommy's words kept coming back to her, 'He knows what he's talking about.' She wanted to give up there and then, never set foot on a stage again, but the excitement of being part of the play took hold and adrenaline coursed through her body until she was ready to show everyone how wrong the critic was.

* * *

It had been even better than expected, with a standing ovation which had lasted for minutes. As they left the stage there were lots of hugs and back-slapping. Everyone was on a high and Megan was thrilled, almost skipping out to hail a taxi to take her to Tommy's party. As the cab made its way through the streets Megan tried to convince herself that this was all she needed, a successful career in acting, and that a relationship was far down her agenda. She didn't need Jamie and she could definitely live her life without Douglas.

'Hey, sis.' Tommy gave her a hug. 'How'd it go?'

'Brilliant.' Megan could barely keep a huge grin from her face.

Tommy peered behind her as though searching for something. 'Just wondered if Ego Man was tagging along behind.'

'I told you, Tom, that's over.'

'I couldn't stand him. I knew he wasn't right for you. He didn't make you happy. Drink?'

Standing at the bar with her brother and his friends, Megan caught a glimpse of a huge television screen. Her eyes widened as she realised the man being interviewed at the end of the news was Jamie. Not the dishevelled rather scatty Jamie with his geeky glasses, but the sophisticated James Booth, researcher in biochemical sciences at Edinburgh University, as she learnt from the caption. Her Jamie had been taken away and replaced by a serious young man in an immaculate dark suit, a white shirt flaring in the camera lights; his hair had been cut smartly and wasn't windswept as it had been when she'd seen him. His bandaged spectacles had been traded for a new rimless style which, she had to admit, suited him. If she'd been at home, she wouldn't have been able to do anything else except sit and watch him.

She took a deep breath and looked away. She wasn't going to think about him. Raising her glass, she smiled at her brother. 'Happy Birthday!'

'So where's the prezzie?' Tommy lurched towards her, smiling.

'I'll give it to you when you're sober enough to appreciate it.' She linked her arm through her brother's and looked around at the group who had turned out for his birthday. 'Had to get them drunk to turn up, did you?' she teased. Megan knew Tommy was used to her banter, but didn't want to be mean to him. 'Are we going on somewhere to eat? I'm starving.'

'Great idea.' Tommy downed the remainder of his drink and called, 'Pizza everyone? The star here is hungry.'

They jostled to the door, a motley, happy bunch enjoying an evening out. It was as if Megan's exit was a deft exercise in stage direction for, as they left the pub through one door, Jamie entered through another.

* * *

Jamie hadn't realised his interview would be broadcast that evening, but was pleased with the media interest. The results of the tests had come in and the breakthrough they'd waited for, prayed for, had happened. On the point of jubilation, he'd been the one who had to burst the bubble for his band of expert and willing workers. It all boiled down to money. He was furious and had walked the streets following the interview, not regretting the fact that he'd ranted to the presenter about the shambles of the thinking behind government ministers when they put illness and the suffering of people so low down on their list of priorities.

Ordering an orange juice, he tried to find a quiet corner in which to sip it and calm himself down. But it was Saturday night and the bar was full and noisy. Jamie left his drink untouched and went out into the street.

He might as well go home, he

decided. As he turned down Threadwell Street, he passed the Pizza Palace where a largish group had just been seated. They looked so happy and carefree that Jamie couldn't help envying them. It must be good to be able to relax and be with friends. He'd neglected his social life and given all his time to the research programme once he'd left the cottage in the new year. That seemed such a long time ago.

Thinking about Meg, he glanced once again at the group behind the window, watching the friends chatting happily to each other. Unable to believe what he saw, he blinked twice. He was right: it was Meg, he was sure it was. He was just about to bang on the glass when he remembered his manners. That was a private party and he hadn't been invited. He lowered his raised hand and was about to walk away.

'Jamie?' He saw Meg mouthing his name.

Eagerly he pushed open the door and went inside. She was on her feet and pulling him towards the table, directing her brother to fit another chair into the already too-crowded space. He was pushed into the group, a menu and a glass of wine were handed to him, and he felt he had come home. Too late he remembered that his dear Meg was back with Douglas.

* * *

Megan couldn't believe he was sitting opposite her. One minute he'd been on the television, and now here he was so close to her she could reach out and touch him. And how she wanted to. She watched him studying the menu, and as he looked up she grinned at him. 'Not quite our sort of cuisine — chefs just don't use their imagination, do they?'

'What would you rather have? Jamie's Jammy Joy or Pizza Diavola?'

You, I'd rather have you, Megan thought, answering his question in her head. Her feelings for him were so strong she wanted to tell him there and then in front of her brother and his friends exactly how much she had missed him and needed him. Just knowing he was only a breath away, she experienced a rosy glow of contentment. An elbow poking her in the ribs brought her back to the party. She looked at Tommy questioningly. 'What is it?'

'I remember him. That's the bloke you were with at the cottage,' Tommy said in an inebriated whisper which Jamie could clearly hear. 'Exactly who is he?'

'This is my friend, Jamie,' Megan addressed the whole group. 'He saved me from going completely mad when we were stranded in a remote cottage at Christmas. He's an inventive cook, a fantastic chopper of wood and . . . ' Her voice faltered. She was unable to say out loud the things she loved about him.

Tommy raised his glass. 'To Megan's friend, Jamie. Thanks for looking after my little sister.'

Jamie acknowledged the toast and started chatting to the people sitting next to him. Megan thought of Douglas. She would never have invited him to join a party like this. He would have made everyone feel uncomfortable, making disparaging comments about the food and wine. Forgetting about him, she was determined to make the most of the evening and joined in the chat going on around her. But at every opportunity she glanced at Jamie. He'd thrown his jacket on the back of his chair and was looking relaxed and happy. She longed to touch him, to listen to his soothing voice as he told her what he'd been doing as they curled up together, their bodies entwined and his arms comfortingly around her.

'Hey, Jamie, did you see my sis in *Watch Your Back?*'

'She was brilliant. Meg is very talented.' As Jamie gave her one of those looks that made her feel so special, she was sure her face was rosy with happiness. She quickly checked to see if anyone had noticed, but they were all carrying on as normal.

'She's not like the character she played, you know.'

'I know that, Tommy. I know she's not like that at all.'

All too soon the party started breaking up. Jamie said his goodbyes, blew a kiss across the table to Megan and headed for the exit.

Megan leapt from her seat and called, 'Jamie, Jamie, wait, wait,' as she rushed after him.

He turned as she grabbed his arm. 'What is it, Meg?'

'Oh, Jamie,' she mumbled as she tried to think what she could say to keep him there. 'The jigsaw, where's the jigsaw? My neighbour wants to do it.' And then she remembered he hadn't answered the text message she'd sent after Christmas. She had to face reality. He'd only joined them this evening because he was too polite to decline, and he'd hardly spoken to her. Although she wanted to take him in her arms and enjoy his tender kisses, she had to accept that he wasn't interested. 'It doesn't matter,' she said as she walked away from him to the cloak-room, where she locked herself in a cubicle and broke down in tears.

When she'd done the best she could about the make-up streaked across her face, she set off for home. The others had long gone. Tommy had completely forgotten about her and was probably enjoying himself in a club. Feeling unloved, she hailed a taxi.

13

The days following the end of the play meant a complete about-face for Megan; *everybody* loved her, if the critics were to be believed. She'd been forgiven for her one-off under-par performance by them and the public. Even her agent urged her to put the experience behind her, but be sure she didn't make the same mistake again. Bolstered by all the positive energy going on, Megan scoured the internet to see what jobs might be available as well as resolving to check in with her agent on a weekly basis.

Her most bitter disappointment was not to have heard from Jamie since Tommy's birthday. He could be excused, she supposed, because of his vital research work. When he'd spoken of it at Christmas, he'd given it a much lower profile, but she wasn't at all surprised at his passion during his speeches which had been headline news for days now. She recorded each news programme and documentary which she thought might be associated with him and re-ran them in the early hours of the morning when sleep refused to come.

The phone rang and, convinced it must be Jamie because she was thinking about him and wishing so hard that he would get in touch, she was surprised when she heard Tommy's voice. 'Hi there. Just phoned to thank you for the fancy boxer shorts. Silk feels sooo good!'

Megan smiled into the phone. 'Serves you right for passing on your unwanted gifts to me at Christmas.'

'How well you know me, Megan. I hope you found a use for them.'

'Sure I did. Jamie took them off my hands. He looked wonderful in them.' She felt heat rising in her face; what *had* she confessed to?

'I didn't take him for *that* sort of a person,' teased Tommy. 'He's a really nice bloke. I've been watching him on TV. High-powered sort, but caring with it, if you know what I mean.'

Megan knew exactly what he meant.

Tommy continued, 'I've bumped into him a couple of times around town and we've downed a couple of pints together. Poor devil's desperate for his results not to be buried without trace.'

'I wish I could help him,' murmured Megan, half to herself.

'Keep in touch with Ego Man, then. He can be very influential when he wants to be. I'm sure he'd sell his soul for his name in the paper in the same sentence as 'philanthropist'. Must go now. See you soon.'

Megan ended the phone call, thinking about what Tommy had said. Then she picked up the instrument again and quickly, without giving herself time to think, punched in Douglas's number. 'Douglas, I meant to thank you for the supper after my disastrous performance and for the way you didn't turn your back on me when I was such rubbish.'

'It's always a pleasure to be with you, Megan.'

Megan could almost see him preening. He seemed to have forgotten that he didn't want to be with her at Christmas. But he had given her the opportunity of getting to know Jamie, for which she was thankful, although she could do without all the heartache it was causing now. 'I wonder if you'd like to come over this evening and have a chat. I was hoping you'd be able to advise me as to which direction I should take now that the play has finished.'

'Of course,' replied Douglas. 'You've relied on me for a long time. It's only natural you'd ask my opinion now.'

They agreed a time to meet.

* * *

'You'll do it? Oh, Douglas, I'm so proud of you,' muttered Megan, hating herself for sucking up to him like this. But if it helped Jamie, she really didn't care. Using Douglas in this way went against her better nature, but then she remembered he'd been seeing another woman at the same time as her and her anger resurfaced.

'I was hoping to get involved with this cancer cure thing anyway,' he said, completely ignoring the fact that he'd got his details wrong and that a cure, as such, was much further into the future. 'It's just the sort of thing I could carry along. That young chap Jeremy holds no weight on the television.'

'James, Jamie,' declared Megan. Trust Douglas to fall at the first fence and get his name wrong; she could have hit him.

'That's what I said. Megan, do pay attention, dear. Now come along and give me a kiss and let's see if we can think of a further way in which you can thank me for taking the trouble to listen to you.'

Megan squirmed away from him after a quick peck on the cheek. 'I think I've got a cold coming,' she said. 'You won't want to catch that if you're going to be talking to the media or heads of state, will you?'

Predictably Douglas backed off, made his excuses and left her flat.

Megan picked up the phone and spoke to her brother. 'If you see Jamie, please tell him he'll be hearing from Douglas about his research fund. You were right, Tom, Douglas is a pushover for being involved.'

Megan had hoped that Jamie would get in touch to acknowledge the fact that she'd helped with the research fund by getting Douglas's financial assistance. Each time she had a call she was certain it would be him and each time she was disappointed. Douglas told her in one of *his* numerous calls that he was now a philanthropist, having donated a large sum of money to the cancer-cure people and how he was now looking for other good causes to support. Had she seen an article about him in the local paper? He had been keen to see her again, but she was able to put him off by using her workload as her excuse. And lately his calls had become fewer and fewer and she suspected he had yet another woman in his life. Meanwhile, she was throwing herself into her work, blotting out thoughts of Jamie.

* * *

Sitting in the coach with the technical team, Megan thought back to the play. She hoped the advert they were about to film would be equally good for her future career, although at the moment there was nothing in the offing. Looking out of the window, she was able to appreciate the scenery. The hills were majestic with a purple-and-pink sheen of heather. It all looked quite different from the countryside when she had been out in the wilds with Jamie. She mentally chastised herself. There she went again, thinking of him. Months had passed since she had last seen him in the pizza restaurant at Tommy's party.

The coach jolted to a stop and everyone piled off. Megan took a deep breath of the clear, fresh air and looked around her. She couldn't believe it. They were parked right at the end of the lane leading to the cottage.

'Gus, Gus,' she called to the artistic director, 'what are we doing here?'

'Making a cereal advert, darling. Okay, get the equipment unloaded.'

'But, Gus,' she persisted, tugging his arm, 'why are we *here*?'

'Ask Patsy, she found it. Perfect, isn't it?'

Megan slumped against the bus. Now she remembered she'd given the cottage details to her agent, who knew Patsy. Here she was trying to put all thoughts of Jamie from her mind and inadvertently she'd been instrumental in bringing them to the very place where all her memories of him would come flooding back.

'Right, people. Take half an hour. Catering's over there.' Gus pointed to a table which had been erected and was loaded with food and drink. 'Everyone to be ready at one.'

Megan wasn't hungry. She slowly walked up the lane to the cottage. It was all quite different without the snow, but beautiful just the same. There was no smoke wafting from the chimney, no snow covering the roof. She wondered if anyone was staying there. She walked round the cottage and tried to look through the windows without seeming to. There didn't appear to be anybody at home. Stopping at the front door, she banged on it with her fist. There was no response. Tentatively she tried the handle, and to her surprise was able to open the door. The cottage hadn't changed at all. The same armchair as lumpy as Jamie's gran's porridge, the same bed-settee they had shared, and looking round she saw little scraps of paper chain dangling from the walls.

'What're you doing here?' called Patsy. 'We're going to be setting up.' She brushed past Megan into the cottage. 'Good grief, what a mess.'

Megan opened her mouth, but no words came out. Miserably, she trailed back towards the group who were enjoying large helpings of stew from the catering table.

'Hello, Meg.'

She turned, wondering if she was dreaming. Holding out her hand, she grasped Jamie's as he moved close to her. 'It's our cottage,' was all she could say.

'I know. It brings back quite a few memories, doesn't it?' Not giving her time to answer, he gestured towards the food. 'Do you think I'm allowed some of that?'

'Not until you tell me what you're doing here,' replied Megan sternly.

'I met up with Douglas at a meeting a couple of days ago and . . . '

'That must have been good fun, but it doesn't explain what you're doing here.'

'I'm very hungry,' sighed Jamie. 'Just let me tell the story. Douglas is donating a lot of money to our project and I wanted to thank him. Anyway, the conversation somehow got around to you and he told me about the commercial. I turned up at the studio just as you were all setting off, so I tailed you up here.'

Both of them looked at the cottage. 'Did you know you were coming to our place?' Megan asked.

'I wasn't sure.'

'Break's over,' called Gus.

'Have I missed my meal? What is it with you, Meg? I seemed destined to starve when I'm around you.'

'Megan, over here. Hurry up, dear. And you others, crowd round and head for that derelict heap over there.' Gus gave his directions quickly. 'No, no, Megan, you're distracted. What is it?' Gus looked at Jamie. 'It's you. Go away, there's a dear man.'

When Megan had finished the scene, Gus appeared satisfied, but Jamie was nowhere to be seen. He'd deserted her yet again.

After a break for tea, Megan was

directed to her place and a shot was taken of her looking into the cottage. 'Something's missing,' she called, just as the camera started rolling.

'Will you stop that? Just get on with what you're supposed to be doing,' Gus huffed.

'There should be a pile of logs.'

'Not for a cereal commercial, sweetie. Do behave. Take two.'

As Megan stood by the closed door separating her from the warmth and happy company within, a snow-making machine swirled out white flakes, creating a very familiar scene. She knew tears were glistening in her eyes and was ready for Gus to yell again.

'Okay, it's a wrap. Well done, everybody. Thank you.' Gus beamed at them all and strode towards Megan. 'Inspired,' he said, hugging her. 'Just the little sad face we needed when you realised you might have to go without your Flaky Wheaty Oats.'

They all returned to the coach and headed towards the hotel where they would spend the night. Megan went straight to her room and wallowed in a hot bath, trying to make sense of the strange day.

* * *

Megan pulled on jeans and a jumper and paced around the hotel room. She couldn't face being with the others downstairs and she couldn't face being on her own in the confines of this stark room either. She pulled on a fleece and decided to visit the cottage once more. It hadn't seemed too far down the road in the coach, but she guessed it would be quite a walk. The others were just heading into the dining room. She remembered that Patsy had travelled here by car as she complained of being coach-sick.

'Come on, Megan my love, time for supper.' Gus beckoned her towards him.

'I'm not hungry, Gus. You don't suppose Patsy would lend me her car, do you?'

'Darling, Patsy hasn't a clue what she's doing. She's had way too much vodka. I'll go and ask her for the keys. She'll do anything for anyone at the mo.'

Gus soon returned, dangling the keys. 'Here we are. Now make sure you're ready to catch the coach in the morning at nine. We don't want to leave you in this godforsaken place. Thank heavens my next job is an advert for suntan lotion. Jamaica, here I come!'

Megan parked at the bottom of the lane, then stood taking in the view. It was the most beautiful place, overwhelmingly so. She walked slowly up the lane, remembering the highs and lows of her time there, and at times she chuckled out loud. The door was still unlocked and she walked in without a thought. The owners would have been paid a hefty fee for today, so she didn't feel that she was trespassing. She reached up and pulled down one of the scraps of wrapping paper which had once been a paper chain and tucked it in her pocket.

She then investigated the kitchen. There were no packets or tins of food here now. The cupboards were completely bare. In the bathroom she turned the tap and the water gurgled and whooshed down the drain. Now she didn't know why she'd come back. Sitting in the armchair, she looked around. If Jamie were here with her it would feel so different.

Her eye was caught by something tucked under the bed-settee. She moved towards the object and gently prised it out. It was the tray with the jigsaw which had been completed apart from one piece, which was loose at the edge of the tray. She slotted it into place and patted it flat. 'There, complete,' she said out loud.

She shoved the jigsaw back under the bed-settee and set off to rejoin her colleagues at the hotel. As she drove away she knew that although the jigsaw was complete, her life would never be complete without Jamie.

14

'Darling Megan, come along. We're having a party. Give me the keys, there's a good girl. I'll put them in Patsy's bag. She certainly won't be driving back first thing tomorrow. Now you must come and see who's joined us. Isn't he a love?' Gus nodded towards the group, which had livened up considerably while she'd been away. Jamie was in the midst of them. Gone was the serious, studious Jamie she'd seen on television and here was the other Jamie, the life and soul of the party.

'Music, we want music and dancing,' Patsy slurred as she grabbed Jamie and twirled him round before planting a kiss on his cheek.

Jamie took Patsy in his arms and danced her gently over to a settee by the fire, where he sat her down and fussed around her with cushions. He looked up and his eyes met Megan's. They started to walk towards each other, but Gus stood between them. 'You know, I'm not sure which of you I'd rather dance with,' he confessed. Then his mobile phone rang and he went off pouting.

'Another drink, Jamie?' someone offered.

'Please,' he answered, holding out his glass. 'Same again, orange juice.'

'I'd like some wine, please,' said Megan, desperate to have some time to talk to Jamie. He, however, was very popular and soon he was in a tight group of people, chatting and laughing, and Megan felt left out and a bit jealous.

She went and sat near the sleeping Patsy, sipping wine and watching the cluster of people. As she watched Jamie joking and asking questions of the others, she realised how little she knew about him and his life. The thought that she knew more about Douglas than about him shocked her, but she acknowledged its truth.

A small band set up in the corner of the spacious bar and Megan swayed to the music. She watched as Jamie flirted with a couple of the catering crew who had travelled up on the coach.

'It's no good, ladies. I can't choose between you. You're both gorgeous,' Megan heard Jamie say. He put an arm around each of them and executed some complicated footwork, at the same time whispering to them in turn, eliciting giggles.

It was undeniably good to see Jamie having fun, but Megan wished that he was enjoying himself with her. At the moment, it seemed as if she was completely invisible to him.

'Come and cuddle me, sweetie,' invited Gus, holding out a hand to her. They hugged each other and Gus led her around in a little dance. 'You did so well today, Megan.'

'Does that mean you've got another part for me?' Megan knew it was the wrong time to ask, but she really needed to know what the future held.

'If it were up to me . . . '

'So that's a no, then.' Megan watched Gus's head shake from side to side, confirming what she'd said.

'Wait until you get back home and put your CV around. Get that agent of yours to earn her Mercedes by getting you work. Now, what I wanted to ask you was, where *did* you find that lovely young man over there? He'd look so good on film.'

Together they looked at Jamie. 'Gus, you'd never believe me if I told you.' Megan planted a soft kiss on his cheek, pulled away from him and finished her drink. Another glassful wouldn't hurt, she decided, walking towards the bar.

'Another of these, please,' she said, smiling.

'I'll be with you as quickly as I can,' the man behind the bar assured her. 'Are you with that group?'

'That's right,' Megan answered.

'There's a tab running. It's all been

taken care of.' He handed her a glass of red wine and hurried to take a further order from another group who were exiting the dining room.

'I wanted white wine,' protested Megan, knowing that the red wine would give her a headache tonight after all she'd been through.

'Sorry, not enough hands, I'm afraid.' When Megan's wine had been replaced, the man behind the bar said, 'Not looking for a job, are you?'

Hesitating for a short moment, Megan was surprised to hear herself say, 'I could be doing just that.'

Her phone rang and she turned away to answer it. 'Hi, Kathryn. I'm out in the wilds again. We've finished the commercial and you'll never guess what . . . ' Just Megan's luck to have a drum solo in her ear at that moment. Laughing, she said, 'I'll find somewhere quieter.' She went into the residents' corridor and put the phone to her ear again. 'That's better, I can hear you now.' Her mind raced as she listened to what her neighbour said. 'I can't believe it. How did it happen?' She shook herself, hoping it was all a dream and Kathryn would laugh, but she didn't. 'But *you're* all right, are you? Good. Look, give me a few minutes to see what I can arrange. I'll phone you back. What a nightmare.' Megan slumped onto a chair and put her head in her hands.

'Hey, darling, what's up? Too much to drink? Come on, chin up, let's see which of us can get that man.' Gus pulled her to her feet. 'Oh, dear, there really is something wrong. Why don't you tell me all about it?'

Gus was about to lead Megan away when Jamie strode over. 'It's okay, Gus, Meg and I are old friends. Come on, Meg, I'm sure we can sort out whatever it is. We've faced plenty together in the past.'

Gus looked puzzled, but wandered back to the party.

Jamie put his hands on her shoulders and his reassuring look encouraged her to tell him what had happened.

'Kathryn rang. You know, she's my neighbour who gave me that jigsaw.'

'Ahh, the jigsaw.'

'I found it today. You'd left a piece out. I finished it.' Her voice quivered.

'Good. That's just what I wanted you to do. I know you're the sort of person who likes to put in the last piece so I left it hoping that one day we'd . . . you'd be back at the cottage.' He stroked her hair comfortingly. 'What's happened?'

'There's been a fire. The man who lives below me was heating oil in a chip pan and had a heart attack. Whilst he was unconscious the pan burst into flames and set fire to his flat. It spread. Kathryn said she saw flames leaping from my kitchen window. The firemen are still there putting the fire out.' She gave a little sob.

'At least you weren't there, Meg. Is anyone hurt?'

'Kathryn said they all got out safely and the man who'd had the heart attack was taken to hospital. But of course no one is allowed back in yet.'

'What do you want to do?'

'I think I'd like to go back at once and see for myself, but how can I do that?'

'I'll take you. You go and pack your things and I'll meet you in reception as soon as you're ready.' He gave her a hug, kissed her forehead and pushed her gently towards the stairs.

* * *

Megan was no longer invisible to Jamie as she'd seemed to be at the party, but she was unable to make the most of his company. He was quiet on the journey and she almost drifted off to sleep. He'd somehow managed to get hold of a blanket and a thermos of hot chocolate and she was feeling cosseted, but anxious. How she wished the circumstances were different and they could be chatting and laughing. As it was, everything she owned might be gone and she could have nowhere to live.

As if reading her mind Jamie said, 'You and Kathryn can stay with me tonight. In fact you can both stay as long as you like. I've even got food in the fridge.'

Megan smiled. 'There won't be much left of tonight by the time we get there, but thank you, Jamie. It's very kind of you.'

As they pulled into Megan's street they were stopped by a policeman. 'Sorry, you'll have to go another way.'

Jamie jumped out of the car and explained. Getting back in he said, 'I've been told to park over there. He's met Kathryn and she's at that house opposite. I think we ought to go over there and wait for any news with her.'

As they walked, Megan took in the scene. It looked like something out of a film. She could make out her kitchen window with its blackened frame and she tried to imagine how much damage the water would have caused.

'Do you want to call Douglas? You'd probably rather stay with him,' Jamie said.

'Why would I do that?' Megan couldn't understand why Jamie was referring to Douglas at all.

There was no time for Jamie to reply as a figure rushed down the steps to greet them. 'Megan, am I glad to see you.' The two women hugged and Kathryn led them into the house, which was crowded with neighbours.

'Tea?' enquired a woman holding a tray of steaming mugs. The man with her thrust a tin of biscuits towards them.

Megan started to shake uncontrollably and Jamie put his arms around her. 'You're in shock,' he stated. 'Come on, I'm taking you home with me. How about you, Kathryn? You're very welcome as well.'

'My mum's coming, but thanks for the offer. Look after Megan. I suppose I shouldn't have rung her, but I didn't know what else to do.'

'You did just the right thing,' Jamie

assured her. 'We'll be in touch tomorrow.' He gathered Megan tightly to him and they retraced their steps back to his car. If there was anything Megan wanted from her flat, it would be soaked if not burned by now.

'It's James Booth,' someone called and a light flashed in their eyes.

It took Jamie a while to realise that he was still a person of high profile in the eyes of the press. The sooner he got Meg home, the better.

* * *

Megan turned over in her sleep and a smile lifted her face. She was dreaming that Jamie had rescued her and taken her somewhere cosy and nice. As she surfaced into consciousness, reality hit her. 'My flat,' she murmured, struggling to sit up.

'Tea?' offered Jamie.

Megan glanced at the space beside her in the bed. 'Did you . . . what I mean is . . . '

‘I slept on the settee,’ replied Jamie crisply. ‘Now, I expect you’ll want to ring people and then go shopping.’

‘I should let Tommy know what’s happening as there might be something in the paper or on the news. He can let Mum and Dad and the rest of the family know.’ She frowned. ‘Why would I want to go shopping?’

‘Meg,’ he said gently taking her hand, ‘your clothes will have been destroyed. You’re welcome to anything I’ve got, but you’ll soon get tired of boxer shorts and mismatched socks.’ He sat down on the bed. ‘I’ve got to go to work, I’m afraid. I don’t like to leave you. Let me get you some toast and juice before I go.’

Left alone, Megan felt miserable. Her life was falling apart. Her flat had been destroyed and Gus hadn’t sounded hopeful about her future as an actor. It seemed as if Jamie was going to be busy and she mustn’t stand in his way. But before she did anything else she needed to go to her flat and see if there was anything she could salvage.

As she stared unseeing out of the window of the coach on the short journey home from Edinburgh, she knew that along with her ruined clothes her portfolio would have been destroyed in addition to her family photographs. She couldn't bear to think about it and wished that Jamie was with her to make her feel better and find a positive side to it all. Now she focused on his smiling face at the impromptu party the previous evening; he'd known just how to handle Patsy and the women from the catering crew. Most of all, she remembered how things had been last Christmas and what a fool she was to imagine that she'd ever stop loving him.

The coach swung into the bus station and Megan hurried along the pavements to her flat, her whole body tense.

She tried to stop herself from crying as she walked through her open front door. She made her way straight to the kitchen and saw immediately that everything there was ruined. Heading into her bedroom, the carpet squelched beneath her feet.

There was a tap on the front door and footsteps. 'Where are you?'

'In the bedroom.'

A willing helper entered with some bin bags. 'One of your neighbours thought these might be useful,' he said, handing her a few. 'Not too bad in here, is it? I think it's just your kitchen that's been destroyed, though there's smoke and water damage elsewhere, of course. Your TV and other electrical equipment won't be any good, but the insurance company will pay out. You'll be back living here in no time. I'll leave you to it.'

Megan looked around. If she wanted to keep any of the things, she'd have to take them away and dry them out. She couldn't face it now. Walking over to the window, she accidentally kicked something. Staring up at her was the happy face of the snowman Jamie had whittled for her at Christmas. So at least one of her precious possessions had been saved. Feeling better, she tucked it in her pocket. The little snowman made her wonder if Jamie was somehow reaching out to her, and she felt able to begin the task of sorting through her things and packing up those she wanted to take with her.

As Megan had feared, her portfolio was damaged beyond repair. Pulling out her phone, she punched in the numbers which would connect her with her agent.

'The advert went well, Gus said,' she informed her agent. 'So I was wondering what you've got for me next.'

'Megan, drop your photos round and I'll see what I can do.'

Megan gripped the phone. 'There was a fire in my flat and they're wrecked. You must have pictures and references on your database, surely.'

'Don't use that tone with me, Megan. It only puts me in a bad mood. Get together another portfolio, bring it round sometime and I'll see what I can do.'

Furious at the unhelpful conversation with someone she thought was there to support her, Megan racked her brain as to what she should do next. In a lightbulb moment, she once again lifted the phone and scrolled the memory until she found the number she wanted.

15

Megan hummed as she polished the tables in the hotel dining room before covering them with snowy white linen. Lawrence, the manager, had chided her about the fact that no one would know if the tables were scratched, different coloured wood or anything else once there was a cloth on them. 'I'd know,' she informed him. After that, he didn't challenge her again on the state of the tables.

Megan was pleased to have secured this job even though it was so near the cottage and its memories. She'd taken a chance when she'd rung the hotel and asked if they had a job for her, trying desperately to sell herself, drawing on the hotel management course she had taken. And it had paid off; here she was with a roof over her head and the promise of money in the bank. She was on a three-month trial, which would cover the Christmas period and keep her mind occupied and hopefully away from Jamie. She'd hated to leave without saying a proper goodbye to him, but she'd left a note saying she had a new job at the hotel near the cottage and reminded him of her phone number. He hadn't been in touch and she hoped he wasn't angry with her. There had been nothing to keep her in the area around her flat, as Tommy had announced his intention of going to Spain with their parents. They were hoping to buy a villa there, having enjoyed their trip last Christmas so much. Her sister was going, too, as she couldn't stand the thought of yet another perishingly cold winter in Scotland.

* * *

Jamie looked at the note for the hundredth time. He couldn't believe she'd gone without a word. He thought back to their final evening together. Why hadn't she told him she was leaving, and why hadn't he realised that she'd cooked a special meal for a reason? It rankled that she'd just disappeared. He wasn't going to let her get away with it and, picking up his mobile, he made a couple of calls before heating up a microwave meal and thinking back to that last evening.

When he'd arrived home from work there had been a wonderful aroma emanating from the kitchen. 'Nice table decorations,' he said as he admired the flowers floating in a glass dish in the centre of the table. 'And nice smell.'

'I thought I'd show you that I *can* cook, given the right ingredients. And I wanted to thank you for letting me stay. I'll pour some wine in a minute when I've put the finishing touches to the main course.'

Jamie sat on the settee waiting for Meg to join him. During their time together at his flat their relationship had been nothing like the easy way they'd had with each other at the cottage.

'There you are. I thought this bottle of wine was a nice shape.' They chinked glasses.

'I could get used to this,' he told her.

'Well, don't, because . . . '

'Because?'

'All sorts of reasons. Now, if you'd like to make your way to the table, sir, I'll serve . . . '

'Hope it's my favourite, spam fritters?'

'Salmon and ginger fish cakes, sweet and sour salad and sweet potato chips.'

'Goodness, things really have improved.' He tried to be good company, but his mind kept going back to the problems they'd been having in the lab. He really had to find a way round them, and before tomorrow if possible.

'Penny for them. You were miles away.'

'The thing is, I'll have to work after we've eaten. I'm sorry to spoil your celebration.' He could see the hurt in her eyes and wished things could be different. 'Mmm, this is beyond delicious.'

'More wine?'

'Not for me, thanks. I won't be able to concentrate.'

'How about pistachio chocolate pudding for dessert?'

'Lovely, but then I must leave you.'

'To the washing-up, I suppose.'

He hadn't liked to spoil the evening, but he'd hoped she'd understand. Looking back, maybe that had been the reason she'd left without a word.

* * *

Megan was happily serving breakfast to the few guests who'd stayed overnight. She was looking forward to the rest of the day, which she had off. She might go for a drive or explore on foot.

'Your day off is cancelled, Megan,' apologised Lawrence. She looked at him questioningly. 'We've had a booking. Short notice, I know. These clever guys have no idea about running a hotel. Apparently they've had to cancel their previous venue for some reason so they're holding their meetings here. I think the minister for health might be turning up tomorrow. It's all very exciting. The press will be here and I expect we'll have sniffer dogs and everything.'

Megan doubted that, but decided it was in her best interest not to disagree and not to make a fuss about having to work. 'What shall I do first?'

'They need help in the kitchen, but I want you back up here at coffee time. That's when they'll be arriving.'

The time flew by and Megan was soon in the small lounge ready to serve coffee and tea. It wasn't a large group of people and they were soon served.

Megan looked up to see Jamie grinning at her. 'What are you doing here, Jamie?'

'I've come for an explanation. But right now I've got a meeting to attend. I'll see you later.'

She watched as he left for one of the meeting rooms. Her feelings were in confusion. Jamie had shown no romantic interest in her when she had stayed at his flat, and yet now it looked as though he'd followed her. She wondered why, not daring to let herself think that he might be interested in her after all.

* * *

Kicking off her shoes, Megan lay back on the duvet. She hardly had the energy to get ready for bed, having been on the go all day. A knock on her door startled her. Forcing herself to move, she opened the door a crack.

'It's only me. Can I come in?' Jamie looked amazingly fresh.

'Yes, you can, but I might fall asleep. I'm shattered.' Megan sat in one of the armchairs.

'Shall I make you a drink? Coffee?'

Megan watched as he busied himself fetching water from her bathroom and mixing the drinks when the kettle had boiled.

'There you go, and as a special treat I've got just the thing to go with it.' He produced a couple of chocolate bars from his pocket. They drank and ate in silence.

'What are you here for, Jamie?'

'Meetings with various people, including the health minister.'

'You know what I mean.'

'Yes, I do. The thing is, I'm not sure where I am with you. We were so close at the cottage, and now we're like strangers. You just going off like that was horrible. It's not what friends do to each other.'

So now she knew for certain. He saw her as a friend and that was all. 'I'm sorry. I'm not very good at goodbyes. It seemed easier to leave a note. But I don't know what I'd have done without you putting me up and helping with the insurance claim.'

'You're perfectly capable, Meg. You showed that when we were at our cottage.'

Megan's heart leapt a little when he described the cottage as theirs. 'Mmm, but it's always nice to have a bit of support in difficult times. I'm really sorry I went off like that. Friends again?' She held out both hands to him and they hugged each other.

'Night night, Meg.'

Megan sat in the chair for a long time after Jamie had left, her body refusing to give in and let her sleep. She closed her eyes and relived their hug.

Eventually she got undressed and ready for bed. Once under the bed-clothes, she wondered what Jamie would say if she tiptoed along the corridor and let herself into his room and they once again slept back-to-back, yet for comfort this time, rather than warmth. On the brink of doing just that, her eyes drooped and when she awoke, it was the next morning.

* * *

'Well done, Megan,' said Lawrence. 'You're always punctual.' He peered at her closely. 'You look a bit jaded, though.'

'I'm fine,' Megan assured him, setting

to work with her early routine of cleaning and laying the tables in the dining room ready for the first hungry breakfast guests. She was conscious of Lawrence hovering around her and wondered if she was doing something wrong. Usually he left her to her own devices.

'Don't forget the health minister's due,' he said.

Megan put down the cutlery she was placing on the tables. 'Lawrence, I do my work as though the Queen might be coming to tea. I don't need to make any special effort just for a health minister.'

From what Megan heard from the kitchen gossip, Jamie and his group had opted for a working breakfast in the conference suite and Lawrence was dealing with that. Having cleared the breakfast things from the dining room and typed up a rota for the following week, it was time for her break. She stepped out through the French windows in the lounge and headed towards the herb garden and a bit of solitude.

Someone had beaten her to it. Megan

didn't recognise the woman and supposed her to be a late arrival from last night or a non-resident.

'Good morning,' she said, smiling.

'Isn't it,' returned the woman. 'This is a lovely spot. The herbs are wonderful. Here, smell this.' She tore a few leaves from a plant and handed them to Megan. 'That's calming. Now smell this one.'

'Mmm, lovely and lemony. Chef does use these herbs.'

'I'm more interested in their medicinal rather than culinary use. The monks, nuns and wise women in medieval times had some good ideas about using herbs and plants, although I wouldn't agree with everything they did.'

They sat together on a chamomile bench, breathing in the rising fragrance blending into the still-crisp morning air.

'I'm Lesley. I'm stopping here for a night.'

'My name's Megan and I work in the hotel.' Refreshed, Megan knew she should be getting back to work. She turned to Lesley and said, 'I can bring you out some tea or coffee if you like.'

'It's a kind offer, but I should be getting organised. I've a busy day ahead of me and I was hiding,' she confessed.

An understanding look passed between the women as they both reluctantly left the sanctuary of the garden.

Soon after Megan returned inside, she was amused to see Lawrence in a flap and guessed that the VIP guest had arrived. She watched from a distance as a large group was ushered into the conference suite.

'You'll be serving the lunches, Megan,' said Lawrence, emerging a bit flushed. 'We'll do it together.'

'Fine,' she agreed. It was her job and she could hand round a few plates without having to break into a sweat like her boss.

'Are you always so cool?'

'Not always,' confessed Megan. Impulsively she grasped at Lawrence's arm. 'Don't worry, we'll cope.'

The trolleys were laid up in the kitchen.

Chef had done his usual professional job and provided an impressive array of salmon, couscous, salad, small sandwiches and other things which would be easy to eat while the health minister was persuaded to allocate money to Jamie and his associates.

Exactly at one o'clock, Lawrence nodded to Megan and, after a brief knock at the conference suite door, opened it and ushered Megan in with the savouries trolley. To her credit, she didn't back out or let the trolley wheel out of control. Had she done so, she could well have been forgiven. She had been prepared for Jamie to be in the room and had steeled herself against that; what she hadn't been prepared for was Douglas's smiling face which was directed not at her, but at the woman Megan had met in the garden. Before her wits deserted her entirely, she heard Douglas say to the woman, 'Yes, minister, of course.'

* * *

Jamie could read Meg's expression well. She was obviously alarmed to see Douglas and somehow surprised to see the Scottish minister for health. He hoped she'd glance his way, but she was busying herself laying the plates out on a side table. He looked over at Douglas and wondered why he wasn't taking any notice of Meg at all. He looked to be busy chatting up Lesley, as they'd all been told to call her. Doing a double-take, Jamie realised that was exactly what Douglas *was* doing. He was chatting her up and it had absolutely nothing to do with the research.

'Break for lunch,' Jamie said and hurried over to Meg. 'Are you okay?'

'Why shouldn't I be? Well, I am a bit tired.'

'Because of them?' Jamie indicated in the direction of Douglas and Lesley.

'What's wrong with them?' Megan said, shrugging. 'Try one of these, they're delicious.' She held up a plate of sandwiches.

'It's always food with you, Meg.' He popped the mini-sandwich whole into his mouth and chewed appreciatively. 'That's good, but not as good as some other meals we've shared.' Last night she'd made it quite clear that they were friends and that was all. He desperately wanted to ask her what was going on between her and Douglas, but didn't want to push things.

'How's it going?' she asked.

'No idea. I can't concentrate; there's so much whirling round in my head.' Jamie helped himself to a couscous filo parcel.

'I suppose that's a problem for clever people like you. You always have ideas developing. Here,' she said, wiping at his chin with a serviette.

'It's not that at all.' Jamie longed to take her in his arms right here in front of everyone. It was as if nothing mattered but the two of them. He'd hand the research over to someone else if he could be with Meg.

'If you're nervous about making your presentation, just take a few deep breaths before you start and you'll be fine. Now, I'd better go and fetch the desserts and cheese.'

As she was about to leave, Douglas sidled over. 'James, I think I'm going to get what I want. But Megan, I'd like *you* to be discreet about our previous relationship. I wouldn't want Lesley to know I went out with an actress who was then reduced to waitressing.'

'Not to worry, Douglas. I'm hardly going to be boasting about going out with you.' She winked at Jamie.

He couldn't keep his eyes off her as she wheeled the trolley out of the room. He didn't want to be here anymore. He wanted to be with Meg snowbound at the cottage. Just her and him.

* * *

On the dot of three o'clock Megan tapped at the door and wheeled in a trolley, this time loaded with tea, coffee, juice and beautifully decorated mini-cupcakes. Lesley looked up. 'Thank you, Megan, much appreciated. Are you going to pour, or shall I be mother?' She looked round at the men and raised her eyebrows.

Douglas leapt up. 'Let me.'

Megan wasn't quite sure what she should do now as Lawrence had told her to serve the drinks, but with Douglas taking on that task all she could do was offer the cakes round. Jamie took her elbow and led her away from the bustle.

'Let me take you to dinner with me this evening,' he suggested. 'I was thinking that we could spend some time together having a delicious meal cooked by a professional, not something concocted out of a limited supply of packets and tins.'

Megan had a chance to merely nod her consent before her manager appeared beside her.

'What's going on, Megan?' Lawrence glared at her. 'I thought I could rely on you. I glanced in to see if you were managing all right and I find you've stopped serving drinks and are chatting to the guests.'

'The minister wanted *Douglas* to pour,' Jamie explained, a smile tugging at his lips.

* * *

They met as soon as Jamie had finished his session and Megan her shift. They chatted easily together on the short drive to the next town.

Finding it too early to eat, they sat in a quiet pub by the log fire, talking happily about their day, as good friends. Megan wondered if that was all they would ever be. Jamie looked so handsome, so capable in his suit and tie.

They finished their drinks and went into the restaurant across the market square. However, as they walked in, who should they see in the cosy interior but Douglas and the health minister, tucking into their starters. The look of horror on Douglas's face contrasted with the genuine delight of Lesley, and before anyone knew it she had convinced them that if they did not sit down and eat with them, they would be offending her. Megan also secretly wondered if the super-charming Douglas was already getting on the minister's nerves.

Before long everyone actually relaxed a little bit. Megan found Lesley easy to talk to and they were soon swapping stories. Megan realised that the men had finished their starters and were sitting in silence.

'This lentil soup is delicious,' Lesley enthused.

'It tastes as if it has tarragon and oregano in it,' Megan said in reply.

'I'm sure the minister doesn't want to know the recipe,' Douglas said condescendingly.

'On the contrary, Douglas, we've found we have a lot in common, including an interest in cooking.'

Megan chose to ignore Jamie choking on a piece of bread.

Lesley continued, 'Douglas, I am sure you'll be as fascinated as I am to hear more about Megan's roles. She's an actress, you know. You *must* have seen her in *Watch Your Back*; she was brilliant. Everyone in the House was talking about you, Megan. And then there was that yogurt advert you were in, and I'm sure I saw your name in the theatre section of the paper recently. I once dabbled in acting until I realised I wasn't good enough to make a career of it. Do you enjoy the theatre, Douglas?'

'It's marvellous. I could get some tickets for the Royal Lyceum, if that would interest you.'

'Wonderful. I'll give you the number of my PA to check my diary. How kind, thank you.'

Douglas smirked.

'People tell me I'm awfully inquisitive, but are you and James dating? I'm known as a bit of a matchmaker. Oh, have I embarrassed you?'

'Not at all,' Megan responded, and continued, somewhat evading the question, 'I was going out with someone, but it's over now, thank goodness. He wasn't a very nice person and for some reason I just couldn't see it.' She glanced at Douglas's reddening face. 'He had another woman whilst he was still with me.'

'A lucky escape! Let's drink to your freedom.' Lesley raised her glass and toasted Megan. Jamie joined in enthusiastically as Douglas took a gulp of wine.

16

The meal continued and by the time they reached the coffee and liqueurs, all four of them were, if not firm friends, at least a little mellower in each other's company. And Douglas had been unusually quiet.

'Just coffee for me, please,' said Megan. 'I've got to be up early.'

'Before we go our separate ways,' said Lesley, 'I'd like to ask you a question, Megan.'

'Of course.'

'What do you think is the worst thing that could happen to anyone? What one word would you single out as being the absolute pits?'

Megan sipped her coffee meditatively. She had been heartbroken when she thought she'd lost Jamie. Then there were the times she'd watched the desolation of poverty-stricken countries on the television. The *Big Issue* seller on the corner of the street near her flat had told her of terrible things he'd had to endure. Surely there could be no one-word answer. Unsure what Lesley was hoping to hear, and wanting to be completely honest about her reply, she decided on, 'Suffering. That's got to be the word.' Now she'd done it. The good humour had been replaced by a black cloud.

Lesley took a sip of her Tia Maria, her eyes moist. 'I agree.' She cleared her throat and continued, 'James, I wonder if you'd help me.'

Jamie nodded his head. 'If I can, I will.'

'I do believe you can. What I'd like you to do is carry on for two more years with your research. That's what I am going to ask the cabinet for. You said this afternoon that you felt it was within your grasp. If you can give a real promise of hope to people who are suffering, I'll back you and your team to the hilt. You have my word.'

* * *

On the morning of his departure, Jamie found Megan in the kitchen. 'I'm going to sort out somewhere quiet with no distractions where I can concentrate. You pinpointed why I'm doing this. If I can move us just one fraction of a step forwards to a cure it will all be worthwhile. But I'll be in touch as soon as I have something concrete.' He kissed her lightly on the mouth. 'Take care, Meg.'

All that day at work Megan's mind wandered, and after a few hours Lawrence was exasperated. 'Have the rest of the day off, Megan, but come back to work tomorrow. I'd appreciate it if you could be your usual efficient self again by then.'

She stayed in her room mulling over the time she'd spent with Jamie at the cottage and the few occasions she'd seen him since. Flicking through the television channels, she stopped when she saw a very familiar place. There she was looking into the cottage with tears in her eyes, with the snow swirling round. It seemed as though everywhere she looked there were reminders of Jamie.

Her phone beeped. Her agent had sent a text telling her that there was another audition for a play in the new year. Then a knock on the door heralded Lawrence's arrival. He was carrying a half-bottle of champagne. 'For our super-star. We saw the advert on the television in the bar. Enjoy. Must dash.'

Megan toasted herself, 'To my future, with or without Jamie.'

* * *

Megan continued to work hard at the hotel with the hope that Jamie would get in touch as soon as he had the results he was desperately searching for. As the festive season approached, the hotel became busier and she had little time to dwell on her private life, although occasionally she wondered if she'd ever hear from Jamie again.

Determined to give the guests a wonderful Christmas Day to remember, Megan sometimes found it hard to stop herself thinking of her own situation. She'd spoken to her family in Spain early in the morning and she had been tearful while she was setting the tables for breakfast. A lot of cards had been sent to her and she'd put them up in her room, but she was disappointed that there had been no word from Jamie. She had no idea where he was, but she had hoped he would have been in touch for Christmas.

By the end of her shift she felt as though her smile was glued in place. Collapsing into a chair in the staffroom, she kicked off her shoes and massaged her aching feet. Lawrence was sitting at his computer working on a rota. 'I've just realised you've done more shifts than anyone since the beginning of December. Why didn't you say something? You are entitled to some time off.'

'Why would I want time off? What would I do?'

'You could try relaxing. You're having tomorrow off. And that's an order.'

'But that's Boxing Day! You've got all sorts of things going on.'

'I'm the boss and nobody's indispensable.'

This comment made Megan think. Was Jamie absolutely necessary to her? She supposed she'd live her life without him, but since he'd disappeared it had felt as though he was just that, indispensable. A small plan formed in her mind. 'Thanks! I think I'll go for a drive, not too far, but it will be good to get out into the countryside. And could I please make myself a little picnic? I'll use the leftovers from today.'

'It being the season of goodwill to all men — and women, I'll say yes, help yourself.'

'Thanks, Lawrence.' She surprised them both by kissing him on the top of his head before skipping off to her room.

In spite of everything else he had to do the next day, Lawrence helped her put together a feast. 'Make sure you get back early in the evening,' he warned.

'Why? Will I turn into a pumpkin?'

'Snow's forecast and I don't want you stuck out in the wilds. I think you're crazy going off to that old cottage. Somebody might be staying there for a start and, even if there's no one there, are you going to trespass?'

'Stop being such a fusspot and concentrate on running your hotel.' Megan liked the easy rapport she now had with Lawrence and would miss him when she left in the new year.

Sitting in the car, she mentally ticked off everything she needed for her celebration. She supposed Kathryn and Sandra would think she was quite sad going off on her own at a time when everyone else seemed to be with family and friends. And Sandra in particular would be appalled at the thought of her being possible prey for a mad axe man. At last she was ready to set off and revisit all her good memories of last Christmas.

Pulling up at the end of the lane, she was stunned to see smoke rising from the chimney. Someone was staying there, which meant that her plans had been scuppered. About to turn the car around and head back to the hotel, she paused. She looked at the neat pile of logs standing where she and Jamie had stacked similar loads a year ago . . .

Before she could change her mind, Megan hurried to the cottage and banged on the door. The front door swung open and Megan stepped backwards. In her wildest dreams she hadn't imagined this scenario was possible.

'Meg? What are you doing here?' Jamie held out his arms and Megan fell into them, clasping his body to her, never wanting to let him go. Gently he led her into the warmth of the familiar cottage.

Sitting on the lumpy chair, Megan fumbled in her fleece for a tissue. Sniffing back tears she couldn't seem to help, she pulled out the contents of her pocket. Along with the tissue a crumpled paper chain and a little wooden snowman tumbled onto the floor at Jamie's feet.

'What's this?' he questioned, sinking to his knees in front of Megan. 'You kept these? Oh, Meg, that's . . . '

'Silly, I know. I just wanted a reminder of the fun time we had last year.' She stuffed the paper and snowman back into her pocket. How long had Jamie been here? Why hadn't he been in touch with her, even if only to send a Christmas card? 'I should go,' she said, standing up.

Jamie put his arms around her and kissed the corner of her mouth. 'Not before I've told you what I'm doing here.' Then he grinned at her before moving away and explaining. 'You must think me unkind not to have been in touch knowing you were so near. But it was the only way I could concentrate on this work.' He indicated a heap of papers alongside a computer and several dirty coffee cups. 'It's so good to see you again.' Then Jamie took her in his arms and kissed her with a passion which sent her body into overdrive.

For all that she'd longed for this moment, the only thing Megan could think about was that he'd ignored her text message and left her thinking he didn't care in the least for her. It was a big step from that to this. 'Why didn't you answer my text message last January?'

His hand squeezing hers gently, he said, 'I didn't get a message, Meg. Honest, I didn't. When you left the cottage, I fed the rest of the Christmas cake to the birds and with the last handful, dropped my phone, too. Idiot or what? Anyway, it was lost down a drain somewhere, I expect. What did you say?'

'Is that why you didn't wish me a happy New Year?' sniffed Megan, cross with herself for being tearful.

'I did wish you one,' whispered Jamie against her ear. 'But only in here.' He tapped his head and winked at her. 'So, what are you doing now? Just passing, were you?'

'Not quite. I just wanted a reminder of our time together last year.' Megan had no idea that he had been so close yet so far from her all this time. If only he'd let her know. What then? She would have bounded down to see him at every opportunity and that wouldn't have been fair. She wouldn't have thought much of Jamie if he hadn't taken up Lesley's request. 'How's it going?' she asked.

Jamie beamed at her. 'Do you know, I think I might be onto something at long last. I was just going to put some results together and see what happens.'

'Shall I make you a drink or get you something to eat?' Megan offered. 'I've brought some supplies. Unless you'd rather I went away.'

'Meg, I never want you to go away. A cup of coffee would be nice now, but I've got a bottle of bubbly for when I've finished this section of the paper.' He indicated his cluttered desk. 'But things are at a tricky stage right now. As for food, that would be very welcome, thanks, as long as it's not hot dogs and a packet of soup.'

'Probably won't be as tasty as that,' replied Megan, heading out of the cottage towards the car to collect the picnic she'd brought.

While Jamie worked, Megan set to in the kitchen, laying out the delicious food and drink. She poured coffee for them from the thermos she'd brought with her, putting Jamie's cup on his desk without a sound, not wanting to disturb his concentration.

The time ticked by and still there was no sound from him except the tapping of the keyboard and rustling of papers. Feeling that she should be busy too, Megan took a kitchen knife and went outside. Not really knowing why, she felt snow in the air and contentment settled on her like a blanket. She quickly found a suitable very small evergreen tree and sawed through the trunk. Proudly she carried it inside and, propping it in the corner of the room, she set to work making tree decorations out of the silver foil in which the food had been wrapped. Pleased with the effect she had achieved, she salvaged some paper from the wastepaper basket near where Jamie was working and cut strips using the kitchen scissors. There was a plastic box with all sorts of bits and pieces, and taking the sellotape Megan made paper chains and strung them round the room. She built up the fire with logs which Jamie must have brought in earlier, then settled in the armchair and closed her eyes.

'Hey, Meg,' Jamie whispered as he gently shook her.

Bleary-eyed, Megan wondered where she was for a moment. Then realising, she grinned at him.

Jamie gave a big smile. 'Sorry it took so long — I got a bit carried away, but I've finished it! I really have something new to put to the team in January now. I'll open the champagne.'

'That's brilliant, Jamie. I'm so pleased all that work has paid off. But I'm afraid it will have to be juice for me. I've got to drive back to the hotel, remember?'

'Not much chance of that.' He started singing 'Good King Wenceslas' in his loudest voice. When he'd finished, he said, 'Boxing Day is the Feast of St Stephen. We ought to look out just like good King Wenceslas.'

Megan teased him, 'You obviously haven't been taking singing lessons this year, then.'

He laughed and said, 'Come and look.'

She grabbed the hand he held out for her and let him pull her up and lead her to the door. As he opened it, a flurry of huge white snowflakes met them. Peering outside, Megan saw the whiteness of snow illuminating the night. 'Just like last year,' she said.

'Not quite. This year we have supplies. There's no way you can go back tonight. Let's open the champagne.' After Jamie had shut the door firmly, he fetched glasses and filled them with the bubbling liquid.

'To your research,' Megan said, half-hoping he'd say 'to us'. But he just repeated 'to research' as they chinked glasses. 'By the way, did the little mouse keep you company? I seem to remember he wasn't your favourite animal when we were here before.'

Jamie remembered as well and gave a shudder. He wouldn't have thought about it if Meg hadn't brought it up, but now he listened for scrabbling sounds. 'I suppose it's silly to feel like this about such small, harmless creatures. I expect you think it's not very manly, don't you?'

Megan was horrified; she'd only meant to pull his leg, but she could see he was really affected by it. 'Did you ever do experiments on them in your lab work?' she wondered out loud.

Jamie considered her question. 'We were expected to and I hated it. Wherever possible I avoided them and searched for an alternative way to do things. At one point I thought I'd have to give up.'

'What changed your mind?' That Jamie was so gentle and caring came as no surprise to her, and she loved him all the more for it. Loved him? Yes, she loved him.

'The Ethics Committee agreed, so I was able to avoid the animal experimentation and get on with, well, helping people, I suppose you could call it.'

'I think the little mouse probably moved home when the weather got warmer last spring. I hope he realised how privileged he was to spend time under the same roof as you.'

Jamie took a large gulp of fizzy wine to get rid of the lump in his throat. 'You haven't lost any of your creative ability,' he said as he admired the paper chains and Christmas tree. 'I've been busy, too.'

'I know you have. And it was all worth it.'

'No, not that. When it was all getting

too much I did a bit of whittling.' He handed her a small wooden snow-woman. Megan stared hard at it and eyed Jamie. 'What's she wearing? It looks familiar.'

Jamie's eyes twinkled as he said, 'What do you think she's wearing?'

'Looks to me like the undies Tommy gave me last Christmas. I must say she looks better in them than you ever did!' Megan traced the little wooden face with her finger. 'It's lovely.'

'It's for you. To go with the snowman. They were made for each other.'

Megan wasn't sure quite what he meant. Was he talking about the wooden snow people, or was he alluding to the two of them? 'She's lovely, thank you.' She stood the snowman and woman together on the windowsill.

'Now to the important thing, the feast! Come on, let's go and see what we've got between us.' Jamie led the way to the kitchen.

After a delicious meal eaten sitting together on the bed-settee in front of the fire, they piled their plates on the floor and Jamie put his arm round Megan.

'Does this remind you of anything?' Jamie asked.

'Is this a game? Would 'last Christmas' be the answer?'

'That's a point. We ought to have a game of Monopoly or Scrabble.'

Megan laughed at his boyish enthusiasm. Here at the cottage he was so different from his television and official persona. 'I couldn't. I feel exhausted. Is there really no way I can get back to the hotel?'

'No, sorry. Looks like you're trapped with me once more. Bad luck.'

But Megan felt as though her luck had never been better. They seemed to be back to the same easy relationship they'd had when they'd been snowbound here last year and she was very happy to be isolated with him again.

'What shall we do, then?' asked Megan lightly.

'I've given you a Christmas prezzie.

Where's mine?' asked Jamie.

Megan wasn't sure what she could give him. Then she gave a little grin and unwound the long black scarf from around her neck and folded it up. 'Here, from me to you.'

'Wow, that is so cool. My scarf. How kind.' He unfolded it and wrapped it around his own neck. 'Now I've got this on, I'd better go and bring in more logs.'

'Off you go, then,' encouraged Megan. 'Don't break your ankle this time.'

While he was away, Jamie's phone trilled. Unsure whether or not to answer it, Megan let it ring, telling him about the missed call when he returned.

'It's working again then. Really, the signal up here is erratic.' Jamie tossed logs onto the fire before pressing buttons on his phone. He shrugged. 'It was Lesley. No sweat. I'll ring her later.'

'But . . . '

Jamie raised an eyebrow. 'You're not going to say 'but she's a member of government', are you? She's important, yes. The research is more important and you're the *most* important. Always remember that, Meg.' He bent to kiss her and she twined her arms around his neck, pulling him to her, her heart pounding. When they eventually pulled apart, Jamie took her hand and led her to the cottage door. 'Shall we build a snowman or be angels?'

'Not sure,' replied Megan. 'I'm happy with the snow people I have, so perhaps we should be angels.'

Like children they raced out into the snow, falling down and scissoring their limbs, remembering last year. Carefully standing up, they could clearly see the effect with the light shining from the cottage window. They both giggled.

'We're angels again,' sighed Megan. 'I could stay here all night.'

'It's freezing,' decided Jamie. 'Let's go back inside.'

Megan made hot chocolate and then asked, 'Do you mind if I make a phone call? Lawrence will be worried. I promised I'd be back tonight.'

Jamie frowned. 'Lawrence? Who's he?'

'My boss,' she explained. 'I don't think he'll mind me not returning tonight as long as he knows I'm all right.'

After the brief phone call, Megan sipped at her mug of chocolate. 'Maybe you'll have to give another interview to the media.'

'Shouldn't be surprised if the *Sun* reporters aren't bobsleighing along here as we speak. And, of course, me and Les are like this.' He crossed his fingers and winked at her. 'Seat in government, I shouldn't wonder.'

'You'll be too posh to speak to me then,' teased Megan.

'I'll never be too anything to speak to you, Meg. You're all I ever want. You're more than enough woman for me.'

Megan was speechless.

'Meg, what's up? You're not still pining for Douglas?'

'I don't even like him really. How silly was I?'

'If Douglas is out of the picture, I don't need to put my feelings on hold any longer. There was no way I could let you know how much I care for you while it was possible that you were still in love with him. It feels as though I've waited forever for this. I did get the impression you couldn't care less about him at the hotel.'

'I don't care about him at all. To a lucky escape!' She laughed and raised her mug. Then she looked round the room.

'No, Meg, another bed hasn't miraculously appeared. We're going to have to share again.' He grinned at her. 'Well, I at least am going to clean my teeth. You can set the bed up if you like.'

Megan stayed just where she was hardly daring to believe that she was here with the man she'd fallen in love with last Christmas and thought she'd never see again. Jamie reappeared and disturbed her thoughts. 'Nothing's changed, then. I still have to do all the work. Come on, shift whilst I sort the bed out.'

Megan moved over to the armchair and watched him busy himself with the bedding. Suddenly feeling uncomfortable, she went to the bathroom and spent some time telling herself that this time their relationship would be for keeps. Jamie was one of the most sincere and honest men she'd ever met; surely she could trust him. What had he said? 'You're all I ever want.' She tingled with happiness. Then she heard Jamie calling.

'Meg, Meg, hurry up, I'm freezing.'

Returning to the room, she turned the lights off, slipped off her shoes and slid into the bed. As Jamie wrapped his arms around her, she breathed in the fragrance of his citrus cologne before losing herself in the rapture of his kisses.

17

Megan was up early. She didn't want to leave Jamie, but she was conscientious and didn't like letting people down. The snow had stopped and she hoped that once she got down to the road she would find that it had been cleared. After a quick cup of coffee she leaned over Jamie to kiss him goodbye. He was warm, sleepy and mumbly.

'I've got to go back to Edinburgh now I've finished here, so let me know when you are home and we'll get together. I've missed you, Meg. Things will work out all right for us, I promise. Trust me.'

As Megan drove carefully along the slippery roads back to the hotel, she wished she hadn't had to leave Jamie again. He'd told her to trust him, but she still wasn't sure that she could. She knew that her lack of confidence in him stemmed from her disastrous relationship with Douglas, but she also knew that the two men couldn't be more different.

Lawrence appeared relieved to see Megan safe and sound after her night away. She felt that he was holding back from asking more about it, but she was going to keep her night at the cottage with Jamie to herself for now. As she got into the routine of work she played scenes from the cottage in her mind and tried to imagine a future with Jamie. They sent each other occasional texts, but they were both busy and keeping in touch wasn't easy. Megan consoled herself with the thought that once she had returned home things would be easier. Sitting in the staffroom one afternoon, she was very pleased to receive a phone call from Kathryn.

'Hi, Megan, happy New Year. Have you managed to find time to stay in a remote cottage with a handsome stranger this holiday?'

'Not quite a stranger. I'll tell you all

about it when I get back.'

'That's what I rang for. The building work is finished. And the kitchen was refitted between Christmas and New Year so the flat's all ready to move back into.'

'You're an absolute star. I can't thank you enough.'

'I think I've found my niche. Supervising building works. Truthfully, it's been horrendous. You owe me.'

'You'll be the first person I cook for in my brand-new kitchen. I'll do you something really special.'

'So long as it's not the type of meal you concocted at that cottage of yours.'

'No, I promise.' As soon as she'd ended the call, she went to see Lawrence to hand in her resignation.

'I'd very much like you to reconsider. I can see you moving upwards here. We will be looking for an events manager at some point in the future. You'd fit the bill perfectly,' he said.

'That's really lovely. I've had a great time working here and you've been the best boss and friend, but my passion is acting,' she said. 'No, my passion is Jamie, and he's in Edinburgh. I'm not going to change my mind.'

* * *

'This kitchen is great,' exclaimed Megan as Kathryn proudly led her around the flat. 'Thanks again.' She hugged her friend and was about to blurt out the news of meeting Jamie again and spending time at the cottage with him. Then she remembered that Jamie hadn't been in touch much and didn't want to jinx things by talking about their relationship. Relationship? Was that what they had? If she was to believe what Jamie had said, then yes, they did. He'd promised things would work out for them and he'd asked her to trust him. Deep down she did, but it was very hard when all she wanted to do was to be with him. Trying to hide her self-pity, she beamed at Kathryn. 'How about going shopping? I'll need some new clothes for the audition.'

As before when she'd been in Edinburgh, Megan spent most of the afternoon searching the faces of the crowds hoping to spot Jamie. She knew it wasn't fair on Kathryn, so she dived into the nearest clothes shop and picked up some outrageous outfits for them to try on.

'You look gorgeous in that colour,' sighed Kathryn. 'Go on, buy it.'

* * *

Megan felt she owed Kathryn a lot, as she'd worn the indigo top for the audition and had been snapped up. Her agent was now a best buddy once again and Megan could have been feeling on the crest of a wave except that, once again, Jamie hadn't answered her recent texts and his phone was continually on voicemail. She felt awkward about simply turning up at his address and hoping he'd be in. She knew he was tied up with work that was important to him and others.

'Meg! Meg! Is that you?'

Megan turned. There was Jamie; it was definitely him running after her. Megan wanted to pinch herself to make sure, but he had bundled her face into his damp overcoat and was stroking her hair. Tears of joy flowed from Megan as she let herself be cocooned.

'What are you doing in Edinburgh?' he asked. 'Looking for me?'

Megan's head nodded against him. 'You didn't get in touch again. What is it with you and communicating with people?' Megan wasn't sure if she wanted to kick his shins or cuddle him to death.

'You're shivering, Meg. Let's get in somewhere out of this sleet.'

Megan let herself be led to a tea room down a side street. Once inside, Jamie ushered her to a secluded booth where she sank down gratefully. While she waited for him to return with hot coffee, she scrutinised him. He looked amazing; even more handsome than she remembered him. As he spoke to the cashier, Megan was reminded of his easy manner and charm. Oh, it was so good to be with him again. Could he feel the same? she asked herself. Why hadn't he been in touch? Yet he appeared so pleased to see her.

'Thought you'd like one of these.' Jamie slipped into the seat next to Megan and they contemplated the plate of cakes he'd bought along with the steaming coffee.

Megan realised she was starving and her hand hovered over the chocolate-topped doughnut filled with oozing cream. She lifted it to her mouth and was about to take a large bite when Jamie cried, 'I wanted that one.'

'Oh, Jamie, I've missed you so much,' admitted Megan, not caring if anyone was eavesdropping. They stared into each other's eyes until Megan dropped her gaze. To cover her feeling of awkwardness now, she put the cake back onto the plate. Jamie picked up a piece of flapjack and bit into it, handing the bulging cream doughnut back to Megan.

'What have you been up to? Any more auditions?'

Megan nodded excitedly and, through a mouthful of cake, told Jamie her news. It was so nice to have someone to share her success with.

'Ace. You deserve it, Meg,' he said, a broad grin plastered to his face.

'Not bad for the start of the year, eh? But what about you? What resolutions did you make this year?'

'None.'

Then Megan remembered the plans they had shared when they were snowbound over a year ago. 'I think you were being a bit mysterious about one of your resolutions last year. Can you tell me now?' She licked her creamy lips and fished for a tissue to wipe her sticky fingers.

Jamie fidgeted. He put his hand over hers. 'Forget the keeping fit and eating healthily. What I really wanted was for us to be together.' As Megan's silence intensified, his face reddened slightly and for a while he couldn't meet her gaze. After too long a silence, he squirmed. 'Please say something.'

'I'm not quite sure where I am with you. After the time we had in the cottage on Boxing Day, I thought things would work out, but I haven't heard from you since I left the hotel.'

'We were busy and in different places.'

'But I've been sending you texts and you've been ignoring them.'

'I haven't, Meg, honest. I haven't been getting them. I've been at the cottage again and there was no signal. The weather's been atrocious there. I only got back this morning.'

'And I suppose you were going to get in touch with me.' Megan didn't want to sound irritable, but nor did she want Jamie to think she'd be available just when he wanted.

'Yes, I was going to invite you out for dinner. I have some very special news.'

'Have you made good progress in the research? Were you *working* at the cottage?'

Jamie shook his head. 'I'm not telling until tonight. If you'd like to join me for dinner I'll reveal all.'

'No, Jamie. I want to know now. I've waited long enough to see you again. You're not disappearing without telling me.'

'I give in, but only if we can have more cakes.' Bringing another plate of assorted fancies and a big pot of coffee from the counter to their table, Jamie sat close to Megan again. 'I like that old cottage of ours. It's kind of special for many reasons.'

'Because you could do jigsaws and enjoy extraordinary meals, you mean?'

'That, and making such big steps forward with work.' He poured the coffee and fiddled with the milk and sugar. Megan waited patiently. At last Jamie said, 'And being with you, of course.' He smacked a kiss on her cheek. 'Anyway, I've been in touch with the owner of the cottage and . . . '

'I see. You can get in touch with other people but not me, is that it? Where's all this leading, Jamie? It had better be good.'

'Yes, I can see that and I hope it is. I think it's fantastic.' Jamie picked up a piece of shortbread and crunched into it. 'This is yummy.'

'I'm going to count to ten. One, two, three . . . '

'The cottage is up for sale,' gabbled Jamie. 'That's why I was up there so recently.'

'For one last look, do you mean? Jamie, sorry, but I've no idea where this is going.'

Jamie put his shortbread down and put his buttery fingers on Megan's cheeks. 'Meg, I've bought the cottage. And I'd like you to live in it with me. Please.' He kissed her, not caring that the other customers found the loving couple so compelling to watch. 'I love you, Meg and I want to be with you for always, even longer.'

'I love you, too.' Megan couldn't stop grinning. Jamie and the cottage. Both of them, together. Whilst her insides galloped along, her brain rolled into action. 'Do you think the cottage is structurally all right? I mean, it was great when we were there to begin with and also when you were there on your own, but that was only for a few weeks in total. Remember the pipes froze, and nobody could get in or out during the bad weather.' Why was she being so negative? Only because she wanted to be there forever with Jamie and if the cottage fell down, what would they do then?

'You old romantic,' teased Jamie. 'Putting all the good things forward.' He put an arm around her. 'I've been thinking.' He tapped his head. 'And I've come up with a plan — well, plans in fact. Want to see them?'

Megan sat up straight, cakes forgotten, and clapped her hands together. 'Yes, please.' It was lovely to watch Jamie being enthusiastic like this, his face shining with excitement. Whatever could he have in mind? Her eyes widened as Jamie fished inside his pocket and pulled out a rather crumpled roll of paper which he started to spread out over the plate of cakes. Adjusting it and folding it to fit the small space, he explained, 'What we need is an upstairs, which I propose goes here.' He jabbed a finger at the top of the page.

'Clever,' nodded Megan, moving closer.

Jamie pecked her cheek and continued, 'Then we can have an upstairs bathroom, and the one downstairs can be either made into a dining room or an office. Of course we'll need a built-in weatherproof container for the wood.'

'Oh yes, priority number one,' said Megan, smiling. 'Tell me more about the upstairs. Is there just going to be a bathroom?'

'There'll be a large bedroom which we'll share after we're married.' He moved his hand and opened his mouth to continue.

'Married? You didn't ask me to marry you.' After moaning that things weren't moving along for them both, they were certainly marching along briskly now.

Jamie's answering smile was accompanied by a chuckle. 'I'll carry on, shall I? There'll be a spare bedroom, here.' He stabbed his finger at the paper once more. 'That'll be for when people come to stay. And over here, next to our room, will be another room.'

'A cottage laboratory for your experiments?'

'Not even close. What I had in mind was a room which we'd need for when our babies come along.'

Megan's lip trembled and tears sprang to her eyes. Her Jamie, their cottage and now their babies. She put her hands to her eyes, not knowing whether to laugh or cry. 'And you say you want to marry me.'

'I've always wanted to marry you right from the moment I knocked on the cottage door.' In the crowded café, Jamie moved away a couple of chairs which were in his way, bobbed down on one knee and said, 'Please marry me, Meg.'

'Of course I will.' Megan put her arms around his neck and pulled him close.

Their kiss was as sweet if not sweeter than the last ones they'd shared. Just as Megan drowned in it, she knew that it was going to be a *very* happy future ahead of them.

THE END

We do hope that you have enjoyed reading this large print book.

Did you know that all of our titles are available for purchase?

We publish a wide range of high quality large print books including:
Romances, Mysteries, Classics
General Fiction
Non Fiction and Westerns

Special interest titles available in large print are:
The Little Oxford Dictionary
Music Book, Song Book
Hymn Book, Service Book

Also available from us courtesy of Oxford University Press:
Young Readers' Dictionary
(large print edition)
Young Readers' Thesaurus
(large print edition)

For further information or a free brochure, please contact us at:
Ulverscroft Large Print Books Ltd.,
The Green, Bradgate Road, Anstey,
Leicester, LE7 7FU, England.
Tel: (00 44) **0116 236 4325**
Fax: (00 44) **0116 234 0205**

Other titles in the Linford Romance Library:

GRACIE'S WAR

Elaine Everest

Britain is at war — but young Gracie Sayers and her best friend Peggy are determined they will still have fun, enjoying cinema trips and dances with Peggy's young man Colin and her cousin Joe. However, there is something shifty about Joe, and Gracie finds she much prefers Colin's friend, the kind and decent Tony. Then, one night, a terrible event changes everything. Now Tony is away at war — and Gracie is carrying the wrong man's child . . .

CUPCAKES AND CANDLESTICKS

Nora Fountain

When Maddy's husband Rob suddenly announces that he's leaving her and moving to Canada with his pretty young employee, her world comes crashing down. As Rob's promises of financial support prove worthless, Maddy finds herself under growing pressure to forge a new life for herself and her four children. She decides to start a catering business, but will it earn enough money — and is that what she really wants? And then she meets the gorgeous Guy in the strangest of circumstances . . .

FLIGHT OF THE HERON

Susan Udy

On her deathbed, Christie's mother confides to her daughter that she has family she never knew existed — grandparents, a great-aunt, and an uncle — and elicits a promise from Christie to travel to Devon to meet them. When she arrives, she's surprised to find another man living there: the leonine and captivating Lucas Grant. But when her grandmother decides to change her will and leave Christie a sizeable inheritance, it's soon all too evident that someone wants to get rid of her, and both her uncle and Lucas have a motive . . .

THE DAIRY

Chrissie Loveday

Georgia is the rebellious eldest daughter of George Wilkins, managing director of the family business, Wilkins' Dairy. Studying for a degree in art, she has become involved with a fellow student, Giles. Following lunch with him and his eccentric artist mother, she ends up moving in with them — but finds it hard adjusting to such a dramatically different lifestyle. Meanwhile, George is struggling with difficulties of his own at the dairy. Can father and daughter both deal with their troubles and find contentment?

A WHOLE NEW WORLD

Sheila Holroyd

Marla's attempts to become an actress and model have stalled. While she decides what to do next, she goes to live in her dead uncle's house in the country, with its tantalising clues to his mysterious past. Then comes an unexpected chance to restart her modelling career — but if she seizes this opportunity it will mean abandoning the new life she has made for herself, and not only new friends but also a possible romance. Which should she choose?